the Siren and the Star

ALSO BY COLBY CEDAR SMITH

Call Me Athena

the Siren and the Star

COLBY CEDAR SMITH

SIMON & SCHUSTER BFYR

NEW YORK   AMSTERDAM/ANTWERP   LONDON
TORONTO   SYDNEY/MELBOURNE   NEW DELHI

SIMON & SCHUSTER BFYR
An imprint of Simon & Schuster Children's Publishing Division
1230 Avenue of the Americas, New York, New York 10020
For more than 100 years, Simon & Schuster has championed authors and the stories they create. By respecting the copyright of an author's intellectual property, you enable Simon & Schuster and the author to continue publishing exceptional books for years to come. We thank you for supporting the author's copyright by purchasing an authorized edition of this book.
No amount of this book may be reproduced or stored in any format, nor may it be uploaded to any website, database, language-learning model, or other repository, retrieval, or artificial intelligence system without express permission. All rights reserved. Inquiries may be directed to Simon & Schuster, 1230 Avenue of the Americas, New York, NY 10020 or permissions@simonandschuster.com.
This book is a work of fiction. Any references to historical events, real people, or real places are used fictitiously. Other names, characters, places, and events are products of the author's imagination, and any resemblance to actual events or places or persons, living or dead, is entirely coincidental.
Text © 2025 by Colby Cedar Smith
Jacket illustration © 2025 by Emma Leonard
Jacket design by Krista Vossen
All rights reserved, including the right of reproduction in whole or in part in any form.
SIMON & SCHUSTER BOOKS FOR YOUNG READERS
and related marks are trademarks of Simon & Schuster, LLC.
For information about special discounts for bulk purchases, please contact
Simon & Schuster Special Sales at 1-866-506-1949 or business@simonandschuster.com.
Simon & Schuster strongly believes in freedom of expression and stands against censorship in all its forms. For more information, visit BooksBelong.com.
The Simon & Schuster Speakers Bureau can bring authors to your live event. For more information or to book an event, contact the Simon & Schuster Speakers Bureau at 1-866-248-3049 or visit our website at www.simonspeakers.com.
Interior design by Hilary Zarycky
The text for this book was set in Sabon.
Manufactured in the United States of America
First Edition
2 4 6 8 10 9 7 5 3 1
CIP data for this book is available from the Library of Congress.
ISBN 9781665972178
ISBN 9781665972192 (ebook)

For Phoebe and Saylor, who fill my life with music

CONTENTS

This book is based on the format of a three-act opera.

An opera begins with a grand **overture**, which is the opening number. An overture often sets the stage for the entire opera and introduces the themes for the story. Our story begins with a letter, a mystery, a friendship.

The next operatic element is the **aria**, which features a virtuosic solo melody line, with accompaniment, often sung by an important character. In our case the aria is sung by the character voice of Magic. Magic welcomes you (the reader) to the scene, invites you to journey through the labyrinth of the story.

The **chorus** poems are derived from the concept of a Greek chorus. In a traditional opera the chorus characters are often allegorical; big concepts such as Time, Dreams, Fear, Mirror, and Bells are given voices by using the poetic device of personification. I imagine these allegorical characters watching Lula and Barbara, breaking the bounds of physics, and slowly bringing the two women together through space and time.

Then we have the **finale**, which is, of course, the last part of the opera. For me this is the voice of a library, a sacred place where stories and memories are distilled.

(OVERTURE)

My star,

I do not know if you were
a specter, or a vision,
but I know
you were there.

A light
surrounded by darkness,
you moved
through the water.

You heard me singing.

In my sorrow,
I reached for you.

You gave me the courage
to know
what must be done.

I leave you this gift
to find.

In your own time.

Bring me
wherever your journey
takes you.

No matter the cost,
the danger,
the fear.

It is time to be free.

Take my voice
and make it yours.

ACT 1

1
Lula

New England Conservatory of Music
2025

The Greenroom

Every performance begins with a moment of loneliness.
A pit deep in my stomach. An emptiness. An ache.
Staring into the mirror. Just me and the lights.
Slowly, the audience gathers.
I can hear the footsteps, the car horns.
The drums are beating. The strings are tuning.
Everyone to their places. Stand on the chalk marks.
Line up on yellow tape. *Places, everyone.*
The only place that matters is here. The stage. This moment.
They're all waiting for me. And I am nothing without them.
Nothing. Without their applause.

Mom likes to say

I was born singing
loud and clear and strong
and I kept singing all through the night
and each day.

A squeaky wheel that just needs
to be heard.

What she doesn't know
is that I sing
because I hear everything.

The siren in the distance,
a train hitting the track, a dial tone,
fingers on a keyboard, a cackle,
church bells, storms.

Each noise has a tone, a rhythm,
a resonance
that lives in me.

I was eight

when I had my first solo.

I stood in the balcony with the rest of the choir.
Shaking, not sure what to do with my hands.

After the first couple of notes, heads started to turn.

At the end of the song,
I saw my mother's face glowing
as bright as the spotlights above the altar.

When the service ended,
siblings, mothers, fathers, grandparents,
priests, and deacons gathered in the hall.

They told my mother what a beautiful voice I had.

Told her I was talented.
Told her I should keep singing.
Told her I could become famous.

For the first time
since I could remember,
it didn't matter
that I never had a dad.

I was enough.

For my mother.
For our community.

Worthy of attention and love.

I wanted it all

Music.

An escape, a sweet dream.
Floating in open water, dark liquid space.

Music.

A raft made of body, and the wind flowing through it.
The beat. The sway. The lift and tilt of planets circling.

Music.

Just a little more.
A crescendo of breath and heartbeat.

Music.

Emotion and electricity. A shiver down the spine.
A lightning bolt between heaven and the earth.

Music.

The connection.

Somehow, over the years

the connection
got lost.

It became about my mother.

Competition.
Winning.

Now I'm here

at the New England Conservatory of Music,
with musicians just as good as me, if not better.

I'm afraid that if I don't succeed, if I'm not the best,
I will end up on the curb with all the other trash
that lines these grease-filled Boston streets.

We walk through the main lobby

filled with debris, lamps, minifridges, bicycles.

Luggage everywhere, some unpacked.

A ship has sunk and washed onto the shore
of a sterile island, with faux marble sand.

Students pull out clothing, search for elusive items,
wallets, folders spilling open, IDs on lanyards, key cards.
Cell phones ring and ping, lit up with messages.

Parents hug their limp-armed kids, cry into their hair,
I can't believe you're so grown-up.

There's panic in the air.

I can see it in my mother's eyes.

I can hear it in her voice when she says,
I believe in you.

What she means is—
Don't let me down.

Mom says goodbye

Take care of yourself. Call me if you need me.
Make sure you take showers. Eat something green.
Don't forget to wear your retainer. Look at you.
You're blooming! This is what we've worked for.

All the lessons, the private choirs, and competitions.
The playdates and picnics and parties that I missed.
And the money. It was worth it. For this.

Don't go to parties. Don't get distracted by boys.

Like she did. She was so young.
She never had this opportunity.
Never had a chance.

Put all your energy into your music. Focus.
Show them what you can do.

She worked two jobs to pay for this.
It's always been just her and me.

This is all for you, Lula. It's your time to shine.

Remember the rehearsals.
The audition prep, the long hours of driving.
The costumes we sewed, the hair curlers.
The early mornings.

Don't forget to rest your voice. Steam and honey.
We've been waiting so long. It's happening!
I'm only a phone call away.
I'm here for you. Just remember.
This is who you are.

This is what makes you special.

I climb the stairs to my dorm room

Open the door with my key.
The lights are off.
When will my roommate arrive?
Who will she be?
I walk through the dark.
Lie down on my bed.
The sheets smell like Target.
The lights of the campus pulse through my window.
I lie on my back and try to breathe.
Why did I come?
I could have waited another year.
Until my eighteenth birthday, like everyone else.
I thought I was ready.
Now I'm not so sure.
I feel like I can hear the entire building thinking.
All the students chattering at once.
The excitement.
The fear.

1
Barbara

Venice, Italy
1635

Mamma tells me

I was born begging
at her breast.

All my life
asking

for love,
legitimacy.

Even in my dreams

I am growing
too large
for this house.

My limbs
wrapped in a knot
around the sheet.

Body contoured
to fit the space.

I am trapped.

Fitful,
I push every boundary.

Head hits the ceiling.

Limbs spill over the sides
of bathtub and bed.

Dresses too long
for the small closet,
where I used to hide.

I can no longer
sit in the child's chair
at the end of the table
eating soft foods.

I must
be allowed to grow.

Even my dreams
are becoming
too large
for this house.

All night I push and pull

try to find
a new space.

In the morning,
I wake
in the same bed
as my mother.

With a flash of fire,
she lights the lantern
beside our thin mattress.

The candlelight
skips along
the jagged scars
that run from her lip
to her collarbone.

I love my mother's face,
beautiful
even with the scars,
and I love
these quiet moments
before the work
begins.

My skin shivers
and pimples
from the frosted air.

Under-dress
and bloomers,
then a shift
dyed brown with coffee grounds
to hide the kitchen stains.

We cinch our dresses
with leather sashes.

I want to pull against
the tug of my mother,
but I hold still.

I do not complain.
I must comply.

Frozen toes
jammed deep into
stiff stockings.

Finally,
we each wrap and tie
a thick
white cloth
around our hair.

Always covered.

In the house
in the marketplace
in the alleyways.

A signal to all.
We are servants.

I open the window

catch the first light
peeking
over the redbrick rooftops.

Listen to the music
of the morning.

A wheelbarrow
clacks along bricks.

Pigeons
coo from their nests,
rhythmic and steady.

The bells
of Abbazia della Misericordia
ring six times.

Buongiorno!

Neighbors wave
from balconies.

Servants,
always the first
in a household to
wake,
pull laundry
across lines,
balcony to balcony.

Exchange the morning gossip.

Men stand
bleary-eyed
on empty porches
smoking
waiting
for the master
to rise.

I can smell the salt of the sea,
a few blocks away.

It mingles
with the dank smell
of the tangled green algae,
the canal,
flowing
beside my home.

The pink morning light
rises higher
splashes
against the sides of buildings
spills onto the water.

The day
has begun.

Someday

we'll have our own house
with boxes full of red flowers

Someday
we'll cook for ourselves
not for others

Someday
someone will love me
someone will want me

Someday
we won't be afraid
we won't be hungry

Someday
we'll have all that we need
and more

Someday
we'll share with the poor

Someday
all these dreams
will seem small

Someday
I won't remember
these cold mornings at all

Someday
we'll play music and dance
and drink and eat

Someday
Venice will fall at my feet

(ARIA)

Magic:

Allow yourself
to take the first steps.

Enter the labyrinth.

Explore
the narrow lanes and
hidden corners.

The darkness beckons you.

Do you hear the music at the center?

The sound of water
lapping the sides of the canal.

Flooded streets
that reek with seaweed
and rot.

And yet, the sunshine.

The angled light
finds its way through
the rooftops
and the courtyards.

Dries the damp
and fills stale air
with a hint
of roses.

2
Lula

New England Conservatory of Music
2025

Butterfly

In the morning, she enters our room.
Flowing silks, skirts, colors,
and patterns pulsing like wings.
She leans over my bed. Freckles and blue eyes.
Hello, she says, and waves her long fingers
as if casting a spell across me, circling the room
the windows the hallway with magic
and air that smells of green grass and clover,
new blooms, forest floors, and tufts of moss.
I'm Agatha.

Agatha unpacks her scarves

into many drawers and pins a tie-dyed tapestry
to the wall above her bed, sets up an altar with candles and crystals,
lights a stick of Nag Champa to hide the smell of her vape.
I'm pretty sure it's not tobacco in there. She looks like
an eighteen-year-old Stevie Nicks who has not been
hardened by years on the road. Music, love, and sun.
A halo of luck and fortune's rainbow aura shining around her,
everything she's ever wanted stretched out in a long ribbon
of a highway, and she owns the VW wagon
to take her there.

I could stay and make small talk

I need a shower, I squeak,
and awkwardly gather a change of clothes,
my plastic shower caddy, a towel,
rush down the hall, push open the bathroom door,
and run directly into a jacked, tall blond dude
whose pecs are as tight as the tile work.

Oh, God! My shampoo and conditioner explode on the floor.
He bends over to retrieve them, his towel barely secured.
What if his towel falls off? What if I see everything?
I avert my eyes and squeal, *I thought this was the ladies' room!*

He chuckles and reaches into one of the stalls,
pulls the curtain back.
The showers are coed, freshman, he says,
and motions me inside.

Why am I such a dork?
A baroque-singing, opera-loving dork.
Why couldn't I have chosen soccer or surfing,
or something that would have tinted my hair
with the sun and toned my thighs?
Instead I am an inside child,
as pale as a ticket stub.

He looks me up and down and says,
I would suggest getting undressed.

I step into the shower stall.
You wish, I say, and then blush.

I snap the curtain closed in his face.

I've never been naked in front of a boy.

Okay, freshman, he sighs.
I'm down the hall if you need me.

My breath shallow, my chest heaving,
I wait until I hear his footsteps, and the door click shut.
I peel off my clothes, step under the steaming water.
Try to wash away the embarrassment.

Whoa, Nellie

Agatha says. She twirls a lock of her white-blond hair
around her finger and narrows her blue eyes.
What happened?

I'm fine, I say, and towel off
my auburn hair,
wishing I had her California
sun–bleached curls.

She looks at me a little too closely.
You're rattled. Do you need me to help you breathe?
I laugh, *I can breathe just fine on my own.*

I lie down, head on my pillow, stare at the ceiling,
unsure of what to do next.
How are you supposed to act?
When there's someone there all the time?

I prop myself up on one elbow, make eye contact.
I'm sorry. I'm awkward. I'm an only child.
And . . .
Tell the truth.
I was homeschooled. I shut my eyes.
Cue the laughter.

She pulls up a chair right next to me,
like a psychoanalyst.
Who the hell is this chick?

You know what we need? she asks.
I sigh and say, *Ice cream.*
No. She shakes her head. *We need a card.*
A greeting card? I ask, confused.

She tells me to hold her vape
and starts pawing through her bags.
Take a hit if you want.
No thanks. I need to protect my voice, I say.
She nods in agreement.
She pulls out a purple velvet pouch.
Ta-da!

Maybe talking to her wasn't the best choice.

We've got to break the ice. She smiles.
Get loose. Get to know each other.
She sits on my bed.
Pulls out a deck of circular cards
with ancient art and Roman numerals
scrolled across the upper arch.

Let's find out who we will become while we're here.
She shuffles the cards, splays them on the bed,
like a dealer in a casino.
She's staring at me too intensely.

How about a coffee to get to know each other?
I mumble. I mean, do these really work?
Maybe these cards will tell her too much.
I am too intense. Too competitive.
All I do is work.
I have no friends.
She'll decide I'm not worth the time.
She'll want someone cooler as a roommate.
Someone who wears ripped, tight jean shorts,
has tattoos, and smokes with her.
Someone who has had a boyfriend.
I look down at my leggings and running shoes.
My pigeon-toed feet.

My mother would be disappointed
with this whole situation.

Just breathe, Agatha says, and pats my hand.
I feel strangely soothed.

She's more motherly than my mother.
I close my eyes. I take a deep breath.
It feels good.

Everyone does this differently.
Pick as many cards as you want.
I close my eyes again and wait.
There's a strange pull in my fingers,
guiding me toward the ones I need.

Agatha chuckles.
Wow, she says as she flips a card.
Looks like you're searching for something.
She flips another.
Or someone, she says with a wink.

What does it all mean?

I ask. Waiting for her sage advice.
Fuck if I know! She giggles.
I groan. *Come on!*
You can't just leave me hanging here.
You have to help.

She puts on her glasses.
They're purple and rimmed with rhinestones,
attached to a pearled chain around her neck.
She looks like a cosmic librarian.

Okay. Hold your horses.
She pulls out the instruction manual.

The Pilgrim The wanderer, the traveler, the apprentice.
The Riddle The puzzle, the question, the mystery.
The Siren Follow her into the ocean. She will connect you.

Does that make sense? she asks.
Not really. I shake my head.

The images swirl in front of me.
Sirens and stars, hands reaching through water,
finding each other on the other side.
A dream.

2
Barbara

Venice, Italy
1635

Once dressed

we hop down
the winding stone steps
to the hearth of the home.

Rossini, the cook,
has been up for hours.

The smell of brown bread
wafts and lingers in the air.

Signora Mancini,
the head maid,
delivers assignments.

Without a word,
my mother snaps into action
and begins to load
dishes onto a brass tray.

Warm cornetti
shaped like crescent moons,
mascarpone cream,
and marmalade.

Thin slices of ham and salami.
Prosciutto and fontina.

Coffee
with whisked, warm milk.

My limbs are aching
from the idea
of the chores
that are waiting.

My stomach grumbles.
Empty.

I stand as close as I can
to the fire, warm my stiff bones,
without getting burned.

Rossini's red cheeks

puff
and stretch
as she yells at me
to do the dishes.

Clean faster
scrub deeper.

I stare at the warm loaves.

No food
until the work is done.

I plunge my fists
into the swarming suds
wishing
they were her face.

I close my eyes

Imagine

I am in a gondola
covered in rose petals.

Drop one hand,
drag it in the water.

There is a man
with me.

He smells of
cinnamon
chocolate
honey.

I lean back
against his wide chest.

Sing him a song.

He feels the sound of my love
fill the space around us.

His right hand rests
above my breast.

So close.

I reach
and guide him
all the way
down.

Barbara!

What?!
I yell with too much force.

The women stare at me
with open mouths.

I come out of my dream.

I've been singing
aloud.

The water is spilling
over the basin.

Unwashed dishes
piled high.

My mother puts her hand
on my shoulder,
and squeezes
with purpose.

*You must learn to work
and hold your tongue.*

Il signore is coming!

Ashamed,
I wipe my pruned hands on my apron.
Straighten my spine,
lift my chin,
and place my arms by my side.

I wish
I could trade dishwater
for the sweet rock and sway
of the Grand Canal.

The women scuttle

to the side of the kitchen

brown crabs
lining up at the edge
of the water.

Snap to attention,
smooth their aprons,
wait for orders.

The master of the house,

Signor Strozzi,
renowned poet
of Venice,

enters the warmth
of the kitchen
with a bluster
that stokes the fires
in the hearth.

His silk dressing gown
flowing behind him,
hair tousled,
mustache unwaxed.

Rossini!

Si, signore!

*Today I will welcome
a small group of gentlemen.
We will need something special
for lunch.*

Assolutamente!
Qualcosa speciale!

I have an inkling for octopus!

I hold my hand
to cover my smile,
suppress a giggle.

Poet signore.
Academic signore.
Nobleman.
Libretti signore.

Famous.
Signore.

Always on a stage,
in his mind.

Always kind.

Makes a show
of every movement
and word.

Turns
and grabs my hand,
and shouts for all to hear,

Signorina Valle!
I heard your enchanting voice
when I was walking down the stairs.

I stumble on my words.

*I'm sorry, signore.
I didn't mean to disturb you.
I was . . .*

He twirls me around the room,
and dips me
until my hair scarf
almost touches the floor.

Nonsense!

I have been asking for years!

*Why are they
keeping you in the kitchen?*

Even though I smile

his words

enliven
and scald me.

It is true.

I will spend my most attractive years
hidden in this basement.

With grumpy old women.

I am
the fronds of a carrot
the twirl of a turnip
the eye of a potato
the head of a mackerel.

Wilted greens.

A servant girl.

Thrown into a hole
to rot.

(CHORUS)

Dreams:

slick fish

glinting, darting

through the canal

under the bridges

into the cool

shadows

tricks of light

and water

pulsing

and weaving

sleek bodies

too silvery

too slippery

to hold

3
Lula

New England Conservatory of Music
2025

First lecture:

History of Music, Professor Jenkins, Tuesday, 8 a.m.

Music has always been an important cultural and social factor throughout human history. It's tribal, it's visceral, it's corporeal. We feel it in our heads, our hands, our feet, and our hearts.

Professor Jenkins stands at the front of the lecture hall, wearing a brown tweed pencil skirt and kitten heels.

Her shadow bounces against a large screen as she pans through photographs of fires, petroglyphs, and huts.

From the first moment,
music helped humans form important bonds.
Music helped people connect with the divine.

Music preserved memory and the ability
to pass stories from one generation to another.
People throughout time have felt the power and pulse of music.

How did music develop?
Throughout the centuries, around the globe?

What do the music from different cultures and music
from different generations have in common?

These are the questions I want you to ask.

She scans the room, makes eye contact with me,
and then moves on.

*The first example of written song is from Syria
around 4,000 years ago.
What do you have in common with that composer?
What inspired that musician to create?*

I close my eyes and imagine chiseled notes on a clay tablet.
The sun setting in an ancient port city on the Mediterranean.

Professor Jenkins continues,

*Always remember that the first instrument was the human voice.
Then came a drum, and then string. A lyre, a flute.*

The creation of polyphony. Instruments creating sound together.

*Ancient music grew in Europe, India, the Middle East,
the Persian empire.*

*During the Middle Ages, polyphony blossomed,
together with a new notation system.*

We will learn how this set the foundation for music today.

She clicks through pictures of knights dying on the battlefield.
Women in flowing dresses waiting in towers above the sea.

Tales of love and chivalry, woe, pain, and plague.

*Then music of the Renaissance, the baroque,
the romantic, the classical.*

*Opera. Jazz. Rhythm and blues. Rock 'n' roll.
Punk rock. Hip-hop.*

Photos and video clips play across the screen.
We watch history unfold in black and white.

Ma Rainey, Bessie Smith, Robert Johnson, Billie Holiday.
The Rolling Stones, the Clash.

Mouths open, faces contorted, as the musicians bear
the pain and pleasure of performing.

My stomach grips.
I can feel the energy.
The pull.
I want to be on that stage.

Music throughout the ages holds our misery, gives us hope.

Helps us celebrate triumph.

Makes us dance.

In a rush of movement, Professor Jenkins swivels and grinds her toes
on the floor and sings, *Come on, baby, let's do the twist!*
She lifts her eyes, scans the audience, gives a small smile.
Anyone want to join? Students laugh.

One boy jumps up and joins her, extending his arm.
Take me by my little hand and go like this!

Professor Jenkins grins and hits a button on her clicker.

A video of Chubby Checker performing on a TV show
in the 1960s rings through the speakers.

Students hop up and dance, clap their hands.
I watch them from my seat and admire the energy.

When the video finishes, Professor Jenkins smooths her hair.
She takes a breath and continues her lecture.

*Music exaggerates every feeling and sensation, until the words
and notes uttered became a manifestation for our very soul.
And the sensuality. And physicality. And passion it contains?*

Scandalous.

*From Mozart to Elvis, Madonna to Dua Lipa.
Music has been blamed for inappropriate behaviors of youths.
Love, sex, and desire.*

She stops for a moment, cheeks flushed.

She walks to the podium to gather her papers
into a thick leather folder.

*The main assignment for my class is a thirty-five-page
research paper. I cannot stress how important
this project is for your grade.*

*It needs to be about a time period in music, or a specific composer,
from anywhere in the world, from any time, who inspires you.
I want you to connect a specific composer to your own music.*

She looks at me again.

I want you to think about the lasting art you want to create.

I wait after class

Professor Jenkins greets each student with smiles
and kind words. I am patient, until she turns to me.
Her warm gray eyes are swirling storm clouds
over a pond right before it rains.

I'm Lula.
I don't know if you remember me.
I wanted to say hi.

She smiles broadly.
Yes! Lula!
I'm glad we were able to convince you
to come to the conservatory.
We were all impressed with your audition.

I blush and glance at the brown carpet.
She continues, *I'm happy to say,*
I will be your advisor.
There's a sign-up sheet on my office door for office hours.
Let's start working on a piece.
Maybe we could link what you're singing
to your music history project.

Professor Jenkins winks
and turns to the next student.

The admiring crowd moves
down the hallway, hanging on her every word.

I can't help but hate them. Just slightly.
I want to be her favorite. Her best.

I reach for my phone

to call my mom, but I hesitate.

I'm used to telling her everything.

Breathe.

It's hard to break old patterns.

I want to find out
who I am.

Before she tells me
who to be.

I am so into her

Agatha leans against me.
I jump. She's so close.

I'm not used to physical affection,
but I don't hate it.

She looks at me and chuckles.
Jenkins is so smart, and she's got the dreamiest eyes.
She places her hand on her forehead
and feigns fainting.
She does, I say with a smile.

You hungry? I ask,
trying to ignore the pit in my stomach.
Please say yes. Please say yes.
Famished! she says.
Thank God.
I don't have to eat alone.

We walk across a wide green quad.
Enter the student center.
It's packed. I take it all in.
Hundreds of people talking at once.
The smell of cream of broccoli soup
and tater tot casserole.
All the backpacks.
People handing out flyers for clubs
and teams and all the activities
that I would never join.

AGATHA!
I look up and see a tall boy,
all legs and arms and sinewy muscle,
striding across the room.

He lifts my roommate into the air.

Her hair and gauzy skirts swirl,
so different from the baggy sweatpants
and crop tops
the other girls are wearing.

I've been wondering when I'd see you!
He kisses her on both cheeks.
Agatha points to me. *Cass, this is my roommate, Lula.
Lula, this is Cass.*

He extends his hand. I take it.
His eyes are the color of a lion.
Dark amber flecked with yellow.

*Agatha and I know each other from music camp.
I play the lute and she plays the harp,
so basically we were destined to be best friends.*
Agatha laughs deep in her throat.
Just a couple of anachronistic nerds!

They give each other a high five.
I'm silent.
I've just noticed how handsome he is,
beneath the mop of dark curls.
Like. Really handsome.

I pull on my ponytail

Adjust my sweatshirt.
Standing next to Agatha makes me feel
like the sidekick in a romantic comedy.

Awkward smile,
double thumbs-up.

We drop our backpacks at a table
and enter the maze of food stations.
Make-your-own omelet, a taco bar.

I go for chicken, a salad, and a Diet Coke,
which seem like a safe bet.

I find Agatha and Cass back at the table.
Cass has piled food high on his tray.
A burrito, casserole, a side of fries, a salad,
and strawberry shortcake.
He's already shoving two things
into his mouth at once.

Agatha opts for a bowl of Froot Loops.
No milk.

Cass turns to Agatha.
I heard Jenkins is assembling a crew.
Agatha puts one red loop into her mouth and crunches.
What kind of crew?
Cass eats his shortcake in two bites.

An ensemble . . .
He pauses for effect.
*To go to a baroque music competition
over fall break . . .*
He waves his hands
and makes smoldering eye contact.
In Venice.

3
Barbara

Venice, Italy
1635

Mancini sends me upstairs

to tidy and dust
signore's parlor
for the gathering
this afternoon.

It is the most luxurious room
in the house.

Large enough to hold
two velvet sofas,
several mahogany tables.

A giant
potted orange tree
grows in the corner,
hanging with fruit.

Richly hued
oil paintings of pomegranates,
crimson juice
staining the canvas.

The bloodred
velvet curtains
frame
the arched windows.

The canal below.

A fire cracks and snaps

within columns of marble.

I jump and turn
my head.

Light flicks across
two figures
sitting on the sofa
speaking in soft tones.

They look like a painting.

My mother turns around,
sharp and quick.

Her dress
slipping
from her shoulder,
her scars exposed.

Signore's hand
slides across
my mother's back.

He's kissing her neck.

A smile replaces her worry.

Ciao, cara mia,
my mother says.

Ecco lei!
Signore smiles.

My mother covers her shoulders,
touches signore's hand,
and looks at me.

We'll leave you to your work, my love.

As she leaves, she places her finger
on my mouth.

She knows I will keep their secret.

My lips have been sealed.

I dust the furniture

and smolder.

Emotions rising,
crackling and spitting with the fire.

Everyone at Palazzo Pesaro knows
there are nights when my mother
does not sleep in our bed.

Nights when I feel angry and guilty
taking up all the space.

I sweep the embers
in front of the hearth.

Hit the dustpan loudly
against a brass bin.

Is signore forcing
my mother into his bed?

Is she indentured to his desires?

No.

I see my mother's expression
when she sees him.
Her licked lips
and soft eyes.

How she turns her head
and smiles as she is leaving.
Charming, beautiful.

These are the moments
when I see her bewitching power.

I place my hand

on the harpsichord
in the corner.

My body grows warm
as I touch
the polished lid.

This instrument
holds all the years of music
in this house.

Concerts
where I pressed my ear
to the door
trying to catch
every brittle, bright note
floating
through the keyhole.

I brush
the inside of the raised lid
painted in blues and greens,
a pastoral scene,
clouds and ocean shoreline.

A siren holds
the carved
supporting beams.

I run my hands
along the black and white keys.

Notice a lined page
poised on the music desk,
scribbles and staffs,
an open bottle of ink.

Lines

from an unfinished opera
that will grace the stage
at the Teatro Novissimo,
one of the new theaters
being built
in the heart of the city.

The siren calls to me

Music flows
from her mouth.

A song
only I can hear.

In my chest,
there is a longing
so sharp,
it feels painful
to hold.

My fingers itch
to write.

She calls again.

I look at the sheet music,
run my finger along the notes.

I promise.

I will replace
the soft down of this duster

with the sleek
flight-feather
of a quill.

(CHORUS)

Mirror:

come to the water

touch the surface

see the reflection

someone

on the other side

reaching for you

4
Lula

New England Conservatory of Music
2025

I inhale, deeply

The Blumenthal Family Library
smells of dust, parchment,
leather, history.

Years stacked on top of years.

I'm comforted by the white noise
of people chatting at tables,
footsteps, phones,
pencils scratching against paper,
the tapping of fingertips on keyboards,
a chair being pulled back
from a table.

A girlfriend squeals
as her boyfriend pulls her onto his lap.

Friends laugh,
sitting close on the couches.

I think of all the hands
that have held these books, bodies
that have sat in these stuffed chairs, feet
that have worn divots
into these stone staircases.

Musicians who dreamed
of becoming,
while notes swirled around them
and settled on the page.

I stop and close my eyes,
think about all the manuscripts,
correspondence, articles, and scores
preserved for others to discover.

I want to read every book.
Listen to every song.
Watch every recording.

Learn all I can
in the time that I have.

And one day
create something that lasts.

My fingers tingle

Searching for what to read first.

I close my eyes
and run my hands along the books
on the metal shelves,
listening to the rhythm of my fingertips
dropping into the valley
between each book spine
as I try to decide.

What do I need?
What will help me find my way?
I squeeze my eyelids and pray
to the universe.

Show me a sign.

My fingers stop
on a thick leather spine.

I open my eyes.

Women Musicians of the Baroque Era.

There's a portrait on the cover.
A figure clutching a stringed instrument.

Flowers in her hair.
Sensual, dreamy, half-closed eyes.
Her breasts spilling out
of a lacy, billowing top.
A musical score curled on a table.
A violin beside it.

Serious yet playful as she asks,
You asked for a sign?

Barbara Strozzi!

I jump
as a librarian thumps a large stack of books
onto a table near me.

She's wearing a hand-knitted cardigan
and a sloppy bun, anchored
to the top of her head with a pencil.

She's the GOAT.

Who? What? A goat?! Where?
I say, looking around the room.

The librarian starts laughing.
The woman on your book, she says, and points.
That's Barbara Strozzi.

I look down, and for a moment
I imagine Barbara Strozzi winking at me.
I rub my eyes.

She's the greatest of all time.
Italian. Seventeenth century.
She was a genius.

I've never heard of her,
I say with awkward hesitation.

The woman looks at me with a blank stare.
Oh my. We need to help you out.
Do you have a moment?
I nod, and she grabs me by the hand and pulls me
into a listening room.

Strozzi was one of the most prolific published composers
of the seventeenth century, male or female,
the librarian tells me
as she hands me a huge set
of noise-canceling headphones.

Many people think that her desire to publish
and have a lasting voice in musical history
was what truly made her astonishing
and remembered.

She types Barbara Strozzi's name
into the search engine
and scrolls down a list of titles
written in Italian,
stops on "Che si può fare?"

Hold on to your heart, she says.

I hear the soft strumming of a lute

A viola da gamba joins in,
a harpsichord, and then the whisper
of a harp.

A woman's voice, low and full,
fills my ears.
The hair on my neck stands up.
My chest, arms, and fingers
feel numb.

A bolt of energy runs up my spine,
fills my chest,
like ripples glinting through
clear blue water.

I've never heard anything like this.
Slow and driving rhythm.
Modern and ancient.
Mournful and joyful.

This feels like the song
I've been waiting my whole life
to hear.

I thank the librarian

I feel like hugging her,
but instead I wave goodbye.

My phone lights up.
Mom.

I don't answer.
I'm going to be late for my first lesson.

I start running.
I make it to the building right on time.

Professor Jenkins leads me
into her office.
I feel nervous and giddy.

The room is expansive.

I take in the large handwoven carpet
with crimson and navy hues,
shelves filled with medieval antiques,
framed portraits of women and angels
playing lutes and harps.

There is a dark wood table in the corner.
A desk piled with papers and lots of books.

She sits down at a six-foot Steinway grand piano
and slides her hands over the keys.

Join me for a few warm-ups.

I stand close to her.
This is a place where I feel comfortable, next to the piano,
with a teacher leading me.

Let's do some lip trills.
I bubble my lips, and then she leads me through
some five-note scales.

Sing, "No, no, no."

I follow her pattern.

"Vee vo, vee vo, vee vo."

Engage your abdomen.
Rounded lips.
Yes. Wonderful.
Create a vertical sound, connected to the body.
Vibrate behind the cheekbones.
Sing into the mask.
And a sigh.
Really nice, Lula.
You have such a lovely range.
Can you sing a few bars of your audition song?

I sing the first few lines of "O mio babbino caro."
Concentrating on the diction, the pronunciation, the timing.
I love this song. I love my voice when I sing this song.
Floating on the high notes, smooth and clear.

Splendid, Lula.
You are growing into the depth of your middle voice.
It will become more deep, more velvety as you mature.
You have an obvious passaggio, as most of us do,
but I can tell you've been working to sing through it smoothly.

You need to connect with the music,
and the character you are portraying.
The more you can let your emotions come through,
the more we'll be able to admire your technical ability.

You can work on this.
We can work on this together.

Do you have any ideas for your project, Lula?

I put my hand on the piano to steady myself.
I did some research, and there's one woman.

Jenkins looks excited. *Who is it?*
I take a breath. Try to calm the queasiness
in my stomach and say, *Barbara Strozzi.*

Professor Jenkins starts laughing.
Is she making fun of me?
You don't think that's a good idea? I ask.
I feel like I'm caught in a fermata.
The final note won't end.
She just keeps laughing and clapping
her hands together.
Lula! I think it's a fabulous idea.

Then why are you laughing so hard? I ask.
She hugs me.
*Oh, Lula. I've always known we have a connection.
Ever since I heard you sing for the first time.
It felt like I was listening to myself, only years before.*

I take a deep breath, trying to figure out
what she's saying, what she's trying to tell me.
I ask, *Does this have something to do with my project?*

She laughs again. *Yes, yes it does.
I wrote my dissertation on Barbara Strozzi.
She's my absolute favorite.
And I feel very deeply that the world
will never be the same,
once you fall in love with her music.*

Jenkins hesitates

We're going to try something . . . just to see.

She reaches deep into her bag,
pulls out sheet music,
and opens the keyboard cover again.

Can you sight-read this, Lula?

My training kicks in.
All the hours. All the practice.
The image of my mother watching from the doorway.
I push down the tension, the nerves.
The expectations.
I close my eyes. Stay loose.
She's not here.
I am here.

This music. So sweet and sad.
It sounds like grieving.
It fits my range.
I listen for a moment, then sing.
Ride the crescendo
and the soft and sharp
staccato notes.

Jenkins stops and looks up.
How did you decide to study Barbara?

*I went to the library and found a book about her.
It felt like it was calling to me.*
I laugh, and add, *I know that sounds silly.*

Jenkins looks serious.
Something very similar happened to me.

Then I listened to her music, I add.
We make eye contact.
Jenkins nods in firm agreement.

*You know, Lula, I have a strong belief
that sometimes we choose our mentors,
and sometimes they choose us.*

*Barbara has a way of choosing the people
who need her the most. It happened to me.
And now, I think, it's happening to you.*

She squints her eyes and purses her mouth,
wavering back and forth.
Trying to figure out her next move.
She places the piece back into her bag and stands.

Lula, have you ever been to Venice?

I exit Jenkins's office

There's a group gathered.
Students who have been listening at the door.
Was that you? asks a girl with multicolored braids.
Professor Jenkins pats me on the back. *That was her.*
They stare at me in awe. *What the hell, girl!*
That's some voice! Blood rushes to my cheeks and heart.
I let it in. *Thank you.* I'm used to this reaction,
but I still love it every time.

Walking home

I want to call my mom.
I want to tell her that I'm going to Venice.
There's a competition. I'm good enough. I've been chosen.
I want her to be proud of me,
but all I can hear is her concern.
Her worry.

I've never been out of the country before.
She takes over my thoughts,
and I can't stop thinking about my future.
Asking myself over and over,
Are you good enough?

For what?
Friendship? Fame? A job? A boyfriend?
All the things I've ever wanted.

To be someone that is heard.
Remembered. Loved.

Will I ever create something
that makes people feel sorrow and joy?

A song that lifts you out of your life,
and you can't go back
to how it was before.

The way Strozzi's song made me feel
in the library.

I pass through halls packed with laughing people,
lines for bathrooms.

Pass cars zooming along the streets,
sidewalks choked with pedestrians,
packed restaurants,
couples with their arms around each other,
telephones ringing, people running.

I sit on a bench.
Place my hands over my ears.
So much pressure.
The noise is deafening.

Success

is a slippery concept.

A swift walk through a stream,
on moss-covered stones.

Just when I feel
like I've reached one milestone
I'm always jumping
to the next.

I wish
I could lie down
in the current.

Submerge
in the silence.

Let the water
show me the way.

4
Barbara

Venice, Italy
1635

I don't get to leave la palazzo every day

When I do,
my heart
is a ringing bell.

The autumn sun shines at an angle.

Illuminating
the brick walls,
white-clad churches,
the emerald canals.

Children's faces
alight with amber glow
as they run with a ball
through Campo Santi Apostoli.

I walk
the narrow streets
until I join the crowd
pulsing toward
the Rialto.

Packed and gliding
through
narrow streets,
like a swarm
of silver sardines.

We mount
the small bridge
across
the Rio dei Santi Apostoli.

Twist and pivot
down Calle Dolfin,
alleyways
that rarely see the light.

One last turn,
and I close my eyes
and breathe deeply.

Finally.
Sunshine.

The expansive
open air
of the Grand Canal.

Gondolas dip and rise

Pass under
the magnificent white
covered bridge
of the Rialto.

I walk the steps,
run my hands along the white
handrail.

I pause in the middle,
look to the southeast.

The two banks of the canal
reaching like the arms
of a woman
open
for an embrace.

I walk
two more blocks
through the bustling *mercato*
to reach
the Campo della Pescaria.

Branzino, sea bass,
packed onto sea kelp
stare at me
with open eyes,
asking to be thrown back
into the sea.

A fisherman fills
my clay jar
with miniature octopi,
folpetti.

I place two ducats
in his palm.

I pass by vendors
selling vats of pasta and clams.

Fresh bread
scented strawberries
ripe oranges
and wheels of fermented cheese.

Chickens cluck
from their wooden cages.

Courtesans call from the windows.

Strumming lutes
and tapping tambourines
singing and dancing
as their breasts spill
from their red unlaced
corsets.

The men
on the street
stumble
and fall onto their knees.

Carmina, the madam,
calls from the doorway,
When are you going to join us,
bella serva?

I laugh deep in my throat.
Whenever I get tired of the kitchen!

Carmina cackles and says,
*I've heard your singing
is as sweet as a sparrow's!*

She lifts her skirt and flashes
her bare bottom.

There's always a place for you here!

My mother taught me

there are only six places
for a woman
in Venice.

The kitchen
as a servant.

The home
as a dutiful wife.

The *ospedale*,
with the abandoned,
orphaned, insane.

The convent,
with the terminally bored.

The whorehouse,
where the women do more
than sing
for their supper.

The doge's prisons,
with the wrongfully accused
rotting in their cells.

My mother does not have
enough gold
to send me to a convent.

She does not have
the dowry
for me to become
a bride.

There are only
four options
available to me.

I can be
an orphan,
a servant,
a courtesan,
or a prisoner.

All come with chains.

And yet

in a society
in which

only

the oldest son
can marry

and all the sisters
have been locked
away,

courtesans
hold power.

They use
their bodies
and their minds

to rule
as queens
of an all-male
court.

Courtesans

free to love and learn
and express their desires

free to read
and discuss politics

free to be
their own mistress
and master

free to enjoy
the pleasures of the body

free to play music

free to enter
the libraries and halls of learning

must also bend over bench and bed
to please their patrons

must entertain
the tomcats, who slink in every corner

must not turn away
from a hand full of silver

must smell the beast
and not fear the bite

must act like lilies
when they are bloodred roses

must never
show their thorns.

5
Lula

New England Conservatory of Music
2025

I open the door to my room

Hip-hop busting out of the speakers,
Cass lying draped over Agatha's bed,
Agatha standing in her bra at the closet,
trying to figure out what gossamer dress to wear.

Welcome home, Tallulah!
I grimace. *My name is Lula.*

Even when he's upside down, Cass is handsome.
His long, lean limbs spill over the bed.
He fills out that white T-shirt.
So damn well.

I bet they've been making out all afternoon.
His hands on her bra, her hands digging into his belted jeans.
I'm not jealous. I don't need a boyfriend.
I wish they would leave me alone.
I need to focus.

Professor Jenkins has chosen me
to go to Venice.

Will they hate me? Will they admire me?
Will they tease me?

Just as I am about to speak,
Cass stands up and says,
Guess who's going to Venice, baby?!
and gives Agatha a big high five.

Me?

I say, slightly unnerved.
Did Professor Jenkins tell you?
Agatha starts jumping up and down.
Holy shit! You're going too?
She's waving imaginary pom-poms in the air, chanting,
Roommates forever! BFFs together!
Cass joins in the cheer.
I hold my hand up. *Wait. You're both going?*
Cass crosses the room, puts on one of Agatha's scarves,
flings it across his neck, and says,
*Apparently, out of the entire campus, this room holds
the most radical baroque nerds.*
Agatha puts her arm around me and smiles.
Welcome to the team, Tallulah.

The three of us

walk to the first ensemble meeting.

The room is loaded with people and instruments.
It's the baroque equivalent of a clown car.

All right. Settle, everyone. Settle.
Professor Jenkins waves us into chairs.

She looks around the room, making eye contact.
We hush.

Jenkins begins.

*For over a hundred years, vocal and instrumental ensembles
from around the world have gathered to play baroque music
in the most glorious palazzi and ancient cathedrals
in Venice, at the Festival Internazionale di Musica Barocca.*

*I have been working for years to get a grant to travel
with a group of students from the New England Conservatory.*
She sighs and clasps her hands together,
closes her eyes. *It almost worked in 2020, but then . . .
the pandemic.* Everyone groans.

*As a vocalist and a music history professor,
I have made it my mission
to incorporate the history of the region
and a study of the seventeenth-century historical figures,
musicians, and composers into the travel experience.*
As she speaks, she hands out a list
of possible research topics.

*Each year the festival awards prizes to the best
individuals and ensembles.*
She motions to the group.
Everyone cheers.

She quiets us with her hands.
We will compete, but I've also worked it into the grant
so that this can be an extension of my course.
You will earn extra credit for an independent study.

And the best part—she looks around the room,
and her face lights up—*your travel*
and your room and board while you are in Venice
are covered by the grant!

I stop holding my breath. Thank God.

Cass, can you stand up and tell us about yourself?

Jenkins turns to the group and says,
Cass will be playing the lute and theorbo for us.

Cass jumps up with a smile as bright as a strobe light.
Hey, my name is Cass Rodrigo.
No. He holds his hands up.
I'm not related to Olivia Rodrigo.
He chuckles. *Yes, we have the same last name,*
but my father is from Mexico, not the Philippines.
I'm a sophomore, in the strings department.
I also play guitar and bass, so I take a lot of classes
in contemporary musical arts,
and I've taken a few cross-listed classes at Berklee,
and play out with some groups from there.
I grew up in the Bay Area, and I'm psyched to be here.

Professor Jenkins says, *Thanks, Cass.*
Agatha?

Agatha floats from her chair and waves, her scarves
and see-through cardigan like wings.
I'm Agatha, and I am also from California.
Cass and I have known each other since we were kids.
She smiles. *I'm a freshman in the strings department. I play the harp.*
Yes, the largest, most awkward instrument ever created,
but I fell in love with it when I was ten, when my parents took me
to the symphony, and the rest is history.

Professor Jenkins smiles and gestures to a girl with pink hair
cut in a diagonal across one eye. She has a tattoo across her chest.
Cynthe, would you like to introduce yourself?

The girl remains seated.
She is long and lithe like a praying mantis.
Hands pressed together.
I'm Cynthe, and I play the piano and the harpsichord.

I can also play the traverso flute, the recorder, and the oboe.
My family moves a lot. She crosses her arms.
I don't really have much to say.

Professor Jenkins nods. *That's fine. Lula? Would you like a turn?*
I rise and look around. Just as I'm about to speak, the door opens.
In walks the guy from the shower.
At his side is the most perfect girl I've ever seen.

Spit catches in my throat

I start to cough. *Lula? Are you okay?*
Professor Jenkins says in a concerned tone.
I'm fine. Okay. Here goes nothing.
I'm Lula. I grew up in Concord, not so far from here.
I was homeschooled, and I graduated early.
I met Professor Jenkins at a competition last year.
She encouraged me to come to the conservatory.
Professor Jenkins bows her head and smiles.
I'm a mezzo-soprano—in the voice and opera department.
Singing is all I've ever wanted to do.
Being here and having this opportunity is a dream come true.

The room is quiet. *So basically you're a child prodigy?*
Cynthe says, with the dead eyes of an insect predator.
I half expect her to sprout wings and eat my face.
I want to crawl under the chair and hide.
I'm not that young. . . . I'm going to be eighteen in October.

Professor Jenkins cuts in.
Regardless of age, you are all extremely talented.
Otherwise you wouldn't be here.
James and Madison, why don't you introduce yourselves.

James stands up and swoops his blond hair
from his eyes. *Hey. My name is James Brickerton the Third,*
but my teammates call me Brick. I'm a football player.
But I ended up in music school because I blew out my knee
junior year and I couldn't get scouted.
His hair droops over his eyes, and he flips it back again.
He looks like the stereotypical lifeguard crush,
that clueless, attractive moron all the girls want.
Singing is just something I've always been able to do.
He flips his hair again, and smolders.
Did this guy take lessons from the Rock?

*My mom went here, so she's thrilled. My dad, not so much.
I think I want to be a music teacher. Maybe with little dudes.
I'm taking a few cross-listed education courses.
Anyway, Mads convinced me that my voice works
for baroque music, and Professor Jenkins seems to agree.*
He smiles. *I have to say, it's weird, but it's cool.*

Professor Jenkins shifts in her chair.
Happy to have you here . . . Brick.
She drops his nickname like cement
thrown into water.

And, Madison . . .
Madison stands, straightens her skirt, lifts her chin.
I admire her perfect blown-out hair, her Instagram
airbrushed makeup, cashmere top, and matching patterned skirt.
Bright tights. Shiny shoes.
Small gold earrings in the shape of stars.

*I'm Madison. I'm a junior in the voice department.
My father is a professor of musicology at Harvard.
My mother was an Italian opera singer, before she retired.
I grew up in London, Rome, New York City.
I want to be an opera singer too. I guess you could say
singing is in my blood.*

Professor Jenkins nods.
Your mother was one of the best, and you certainly take after her.

My blood pumps harder

I think about my mother singing.

In the shower, at stoplights,
while she's folding laundry.

So confident, powerful, beautiful.

I never knew my father.

Now I wonder
if I have ever really known
my mom.

Could she have been
one of the best?

If she hadn't gotten pregnant
her senior year
and dropped out of her life
to make a life
for me?

Jenkins tells us to stand

Huddle up, she says.

We link arms in a tight circle.

I have been searching for the perfect group for a very long time.
I want you to know that you have been hand selected.
And I think, if we can learn to work together as a team,
we will be unstoppable.

And, she says with a grin,
we're going to have the time of our lives!

I look around the room at the shining faces

Wasn't it Groucho Marx who said,
I never want to join a group that would have me as a member?
For all these years, I have lived by this manifesto.
If I'm being completely honest, no group has ever invited me to join.
I've always been the weirdo on the edge of the playground.
The pigeon pecking on crumbs. Minding its own business.
And that's been okay. I've never needed anyone or anything.
Except music, and my mom. Now I'm standing
in this room, staring at Jenkins's infectious grin.
Cass's wide smile to my left, Agatha's bouncing curls to my right.
All this cheering and smiling and excitement has gotten to me.
Instead of ignoring them, or competing against them,
I want to compete with them.
I want to belong to this group of freaks.

5
Barbara

Venice, Italy
1635

I love

the crowded streets

and the dark,
quiet corners.

Where I can breathe
and be alone.

No one listening
except the water
rushing beside me.

I place one hand
on my belly,
one hand
on my heart.

I sing a folk song
I've heard in the kitchen.

Ma come balli bella bimba,
bella bimba, bella bimba.
Ma come balli bella bimba,
bella bimba, balli ben!

The corners of my mouth turn up,
my chest bounces
as the words and the breath
hit my body.

My throat glides along the notes.

I feel giddy,
body full
of air and sound.

Danza al mattino,
Danza alla sera,
Sempre leggera,
Sembra volar!

I stand and curtsy
to a group of pigeons
feasting on abandoned
breadcrumbs.

Hold my arms up,
as if I am being held
by a partner.

My feet begin to glide
across the stones.

I turn around,
laughing
as I bend
to address the flock.

Together
they scatter and lift,
pulse
their way
into the sky.

I hear the bell tower ringing

that old nagging
grandfather
always telling us what to do.

Once again
I have been lost
in my music and dreams.

Rossini
will knock me on the knuckles
with a wooden spoon
if I don't get her these ingredients
in time
for signore's guests.

I can feel
the *folpetti*
trying to escape
from the clay pot
in my basket.

I tap it down.
Seal them in.

Begin to run
toward home.

I turn a corner

barrel into three men
carrying stacks
of papers.

The white sheets
fly everywhere.

Fruit rolls across the cobblestone.

The clay pot holding the octopi
cracks on the ground.

Purple-gray flesh oozes
out in a mercurial glob.

I see a tentacle inch forward.
Sepia ink spills
into the cracks.

Thank God. Still alive.

I rush to grab them before they escape,
place their wet bodies
in the basket.

A hand grabs me,
pulls me to my feet,
and shoves me against
a building.

Bastarda!
Watch where you're going!

His eyes look dead.

Ferrante!
Leave her be!

I try to run.

He grabs my hand hard
and twists it
behind my back.

*Shut up, Nicolò.
I'm teaching this servant girl
a lesson.*

I wiggle,
and try to pry
myself away.

*Stop! Ferrante!
Can't you see who she is?
Look at her uniform.
She works for Signor Strozzi.*

*He won't be pleased if you murder
his kitchen maid
before she serves you lunch.*

Loredano! Tell him!

Loredano
smiles, pats his friend
on the back,
and takes a swig
from a flask of ale.

*We have better things to do, Ferrante.
It's best not to fight with the servants.*

Ferrante releases me.
He spits on my shoe.

Pick this up, bastarda!

I kneel to pick up the papers
that have flown in every direction.

They watch me
gather each page and smooth it.

I notice that
they're not letters.

They're notes.

A swift canal
of dots and arches
swirling across the page.

Nicolò
walks a few paces,
retrieves the pages
that have fluttered down the alley.

He adds them to my stack.

Is this music? I ask,
not taking my eyes from
the swirling eddies,
the river of lines
that somehow
turn into sound.

    Yes. I wrote it.

I raise my eyes
and look at him.

I see a young man
with dark brown hair,
eyes the color of olives.

What a gift, I say.

His eyes widen,
and his voice hardens.

   It's not a gift for anyone.

*I meant, what a gift
to be able to read.*

He looks at me
with pity.
His mouth opens
but no sound escapes.

*Nicolò! Stop it!
Leave the* bastarda!
We're late.

The three men turn,
walk away
without looking back.

I know my letters

I want to tell him.

My mother taught me
how to read
by the candlelight
in our room.

Simple words
I need to know in the market.

I can do a little math.

What I need to survive.

I touch my shoulders,
explore the damage
with my fingers.

Feel the anger
bruising my skin.

I've never touched a book.

Or written anything.

The thought of it
makes my hands twitch.

The siren hands me a feather,
dipped in ink.

I could write.

All my thoughts.
All my songs.

Bastarda

A girl without a father.

Bastarda

A girl without a name.

Bastarda

A girl who serves a master.

Bastarda

A girl who asks her mother.

Bastarda

A mother who refuses to tell.

(CHORUS)

Dreams:

Out of the muck

and the mire

we are silk

and desire

we will always

give you more

than you

ask for

6
Lula

New England Conservatory of Music
2025

Everyone, gather together!

We all stand in a circle.
Raise your hands to the air. Inhale. Close your eyes.
Jenkins reaches into the air.
Extend your spinal cord.
Find the air and space between your vertebrae.
Drop down, exhale, touch your toes to the ground.

She eyes Brick stretching halfway,
his thighs the size of timpani drums, and adds,
If you can. Brick laughs. *Lady, I'm a baller,*
not a ballerina.

Jenkins ignores him. *Lift up once again*
and inhale through your nostrils.
We all do as we're told.
Now bend your knees slightly and center yourself.
Roll your neck and release all the tension.

I try, but I can't release anything. I'm too nervous.
I just want to begin. I want to prove that Jenkins
didn't make a mistake. I'm supposed to be here.

Jenkins continues,
No matter what instrument you play,
we all need to be grounded.
She puts one hand to her chest, the other on her stomach.
Body, mind, and spirit. Connected.

We all follow her and place our hands
on our centers and hearts.

If we can do this, we can open ourselves to the music.

I want everyone to think

*deeply about your projects and what songs you want
to bring to the group. Does anyone have ideas?*
Madison's hand shoots up.
I want to slap her hand down and raise mine instead.

Yes, Madison?
She breathes in sharply and says,
*I want to study early opera.
It's unique to Venice and the period we're studying.*

Jenkins smiles. *I think that's a great idea, Madison.
Lula is also linking her project to Venice.
She'll be studying composer Barbara Strozzi.*

Sweat forms on my brow.
My stomach feels like it's dropped down to my shoes.
Madison shoots daggers from her eyes.

Jenkins turns to Cynthe and Agatha and Cass.
*I would really love to do one instrumental piece
that concentrates on the level of musicianship
that you three can offer. Can you choose a piece?*
They nod in unison. *Anyone else have any ideas?*

Brick sighs. *I'm still trying to find something
that I can connect with, emotionally.*
We all stare at him.
What? I have a heart! he shouts.
Cynthe stares into the empty cavern of Brick's chest.
Madison pats him on the back. *Of course you do.*

That's great, Brick, Jenkins adds.
*I'm happy you're trying to connect.
I'm sure you ALL will choose something wonderful.*

I push down the bile that's rising in my throat.

Agatha leans toward me

I'm going to Berklee to watch Cass play in a jazz ensemble.
Want to come? I look at my pigeon toes.
With every fiber of my being,
I want to go back to the room.
I want to get lost in my research.

Just try. Make friends,
I tell my inner child,
overwhelmed and alone,
sad in the corner of the playground.

Sure, I say with a shrug.
She clasps her hands together.
It'll be great!
We can make fun of Cass.
He gets all cool and less nerdy with the Berklee crew.
It's hilarious to watch.
Plus, we can go to my favorite bar.

Bar? I croak.
Yes. She nods enthusiastically and adds,
They have great burgers!
I try to calm myself, but my heart is flip-flopping.
I don't have a fake ID, I say.
I'm relieved I can't go.
No probs! she says.
They don't ID cute young girls!
I shoot her a horrified expression, trying to figure out
if I should explain that her response only makes it worse.

Before I can protest, we're walking up Mass Avenue,
heading toward Boylston Street
and the beating drum of Berklee College of Music.

We crowd

into the David Friend Recital Hall on Boylston Street.
Cass looks elated playing jazz.
My neck tingles as I watch him move
his long, muscular limbs to the beat of the snare.
His brown skin against a crisp white shirt.
He's beautiful. Glowing under the spotlight.
In the pocket of the groove,
his lips curl in a joyful expression,
he closes his eyes and pulses,
running licks on the guitar.
Passing it off to the saxophonist, the pianist, the bass.
It's foot-tapping music, smooth and breezy,
the high hat ringing my spine.
I have to sit on my hands.
I want to jump up and join them.
The piano pulses the first notes of
"I Fall in Love Too Easily."
Cass's fingers press and slide along the neck
as a trumpet laments and sways behind him.
He makes eye contact with me, and smiles.
My chest swells with heat and rhythm.
What will it feel like to play music with Cass?
The low register, gliding across velvet,
the way my voice could snake through these notes,
through his fingers on the strings
like a cat rubbing its back on exposed skin,
a tail curling around a bare ankle.

After the concert

we walk through a crowd of smokers
outside of Bukowski's.
I use my hand as a fan.
I would do anything to protect my voice,
and these people are killing themselves.

I'm still coughing when we find a small table,
sticky with years of spilled beer and ketchup
and who the hell knows what else.

I stare at one of the many framed Bukowski quotes
on the wall, and a black-and-white picture
of the captain himself. He tips his hat
and tells me in a whiskey-stained voice,
Find what you love, and let it kill you.

The waitress stands by our table,
and Agatha orders a burger and a beer.
My voice cracks when I say,
I'll have the same.
The waitress grins and pops her gum.
Coming right up, ladies.

When the food arrives, steaming
and smelling like a carnival, Agatha takes a bite,
licks sauce from her lip, and says,
I adore this place. It feels so . . . Boston.

I take a bite of my cheeseburger and a large swig
of a Blue Moon draft, and I must admit,
it's a damn good combo,
and there's something about these quotes
on the wall that are hitting hard.
I wanted the whole world or nothing.

When I look up from my fries,
I see Cass striding through the door.
Confidently fist-bumping and bro hugging
people he recognizes in the bar.
Agatha jumps up and hugs him, and tells him,
You were phenomenal! He looks at me and says,
Tallulah! You came!

I smile at him, and stare at the quote behind his head.

Your eyes—they're beautiful.
They're wild, crazy, like some animal
peering out of a forest on fire.

Cass sits next to me

Puts his arm around me.
Leans in.

Now that he's closer,
I can see that his eyes are light brown,
with flecks of yellow and mahogany.

They're joyful.
A boy peering out from a man's
chiseled face.

I smell his deodorant, citrus and spice.
Breathe in.

Admire the peppering of freckles,
the way his dark hair curls
around his earlobe.

I can't wait to play music together, he says.

Maybe it's the commotion of the bar,
or the warmth of the beer,
but I want to lean in
closer,
and kiss him.

I look at Agatha across from us.
She's smiling too.

Does she see my attraction?
Does she hate me?
I take a sip of my drink,
but my hand shakes.

You two are lucky to have each other,
I say, trying to not expose my jealousy.
My desire for someone to love me.
Someone like Cass.

I don't know what I'd do without you,
Agatha says to Cass, and leans across the table.
Kisses him on the cheek.

Ditto, he says, taking his arm from my shoulder,
reaching across the table to hold her hand.

My whole body aches for him.

I want him to bring his arms back
and wrap them around me.

I look at Agatha smiling, face open,
full of admiration.

I love you both, she says,
and places one hand on his cheek,
and one hand on mine.

I know it's the beer talking,
but I feel the same.

If Cass can't love me,
I'm glad he's given his heart
to someone as glorious
as Agatha.

6
Barbara

Venice, Italy
1635

A knock on the door

fills my body with dread.

I will have to see them again.

Ferrante,
angry and violent.

Nicolò,
rich and complicit.

Loredano,
cool and filled
with distain.

I wish I could greet them
at the door
with a fist.

Instead I peel off
my dirty kitchen apron.

Swallow
a mouthful of angry acid
and open the door.

It's a man
that I don't recognize.

Benvenuto, vieni pure,
I say with a smile
as I take his blue velvet cloak
and feathered cap.

I usher him
into the parlor
and pour him a goblet of wine.

After I greet a few more guests,
I rush back to the kitchen
to help with last-minute
food preparations.

Rossini's red cheeks
are hotter than usual.

Mancini lays out
glassware and silver.

My mother loads
food onto trays.

The *folpetti*
shiver on a silver dish.

Served cold
with olive oil, salt and pepper
shaved celery
and lemon.

Nothing to take away
the taste of the sea.

Mussels
packed with breadcrumbs
parsley and parmesan
make my mouth water.

I want to pluck one
off the plate,
place the symphony of flavor
in my mouth,
but I know Rossini
would have a fit.

A final knock.
My stomach shrinks.

I run back upstairs,
wiping my soiled hands on my apron,
before I reach for the handle.

Hello, bastarda*!*
Ferrante stands at the door,
smiling.

Leave her alone

Nicolò pushes
Ferrante aside.

The three men
fill the entryway.

Hello again, Nicolò says,
and cracks a smile.

Don't worry about him.
I've told him to behave.

Loredano,
formal and stiff,
holds out his jacket
without a smile.

Silently
I take their hats and cloaks,
and lead them to the parlor.

I do not offer them
words, nor wine.

I want them to know
they are not
welcome here.

I know I shouldn't spy

I can't help it.

My body is hungry,
and my mind is voracious.

I want to eat the words
that seep through this keyhole.

Tear into
the horrible, damaging phrases
that float
from the mouths of men.

These geniuses.
These giants of art and industry.
Senators and writers.
Noblemen.
Abusers, home-wreckers.
These liars.

Should be knocked from their pedestals.

Their medals
stripped from their necks.

A deep voice is noble

*A man's body, by design,
is a large cavity,
strong, warm in nature.*

*A woman's body is too weak, too moist.
Generally out of control.*

Through the keyhole,
I can make out the silhouette
of one man pacing in front of the room.

He leans against the fireplace
with a pipe in his hand.

The other hand, on his hip,
holding his silk waistcoat to the side.

They have started a debate.

Drinking
strong grappa,
smoking,
admonishing women.

*Girls, women
have cold bodies
that produce small amounts
of air at too rapid a speed.*

*Their throats are small.
They are hard and not flexible.*

These voices do not please.

*Women are filled with
sharpness and glitter,
like the jewels
they wear around their necks.*

Another man in the group stands.
I agree.

*A man's voice can move from highest to lowest.
He can bend and twist, like the softest of wax
whenever he wishes.*

I recognize Ferrante's voice
as he stands and says,

Bodies make and receive music.

*When a woman does fantastic things
with her mouth and throat,
she taunts us!*

She cannot control herself!

*And we men can think of nothing else
but her lips and her tongue.*

*I, for one,
do not welcome women
on the public stage.*

*They are better cloistered
in convents, and palaces.*

*It is better for a man
to play the role of a woman.*

*Or to have a whore
sing to us,
so we can pay her
for her song and services.*

It's less complicated for all.

Loredano stands and laughs.

*And what
of the castrati?*

*Cut to induce the sound of a woman
in the body of a man?*

*What say you of the merit
of their voices?*

A voice calls from the back,

*Although high,
the voice still flows
through the body of a man,
and contains the agility and warmth
of the masculine frame.*

Ferrante thrusts his hips.
And castrati can still give us pleasure!

Nicolò stands,
silences the eruption
of laughter
with his palms
in the air.

*I don't even think a common woman
or a noblewoman
could achieve*

*the sensuality or passion
that is needed on the stage.*

*How can they produce a sound
that would make us feel desire
or pain?*

They know nothing of the world.

Ferrante cuts in.

*Leave the music to the cut
and the damaged.*

The castrati and the courtesans.

*They please us,
because they have known
the power
of a man's unsheathed knife.*

The other men chortle.

They laugh
at the violence they commit.

Bile rises in my throat.

I cannot take
much more of this.

I throw open the door.

Women can sing as well as men

Of course,
you wouldn't know it,
because you never allow us the chance!

We are only allowed
to sing behind veils
and metal grates in churches
because you do not acknowledge
that we exist!

Open-mouthed faces
stare at me,
in shock.

I close my eyes, clench my fist,
and yell,

We are sheltered.
Imprisoned in our palaces, cells,
and kitchens.

We are locked away,
forgotten,
and you hold the key!

Even boys
are mutilated to become
something you desire!

I open my eyes,
feel the anger boiling in the room.

All the men
rise to their feet.

Signore standing
at the back of the room.

Frozen
holding a cup of tea
suspended in midair.

Shock and disappointment
spill from his eyes
and open mouth.

Their privacy disturbed
by a girl wearing an apron,
holding a knife
in her hand.

(CHORUS)

Magic:

a shiver

a dream

all that is not seen

that's how

you save a life

a siren

a knife

a reaching hand

to stir the pot

the weeping willow

ties the knot

a thread to break

a thread to mend

one little wish

and time

will bend

7
Lula

New England Conservatory of Music
2025

Professor Jenkins presses her fingers

hard into the keys.
They bounce like tiny firecrackers.
She hits the staccato notes.
Tick, tick, tick.
A human metronome.
Keeping me on time, keeping me on earth.
My voice lilts and lifts, separates each phrase.
I rock onto my toes, careful not to fall flat.
Float above the note.
My mouth soft and round, my eyebrows raised.
She makes eye contact to signal.
We are in the final measures.
Her full hands fierce on the last chords.
Pop. Pop. Pop.
I fly high above.

Truly beautiful, Lula

she says to me, and pats the chair
beside the piano bench. I sit next to her.
*Have you chosen which one of Barbara's songs
to sing at the festival?*

I nod and say, *Maybe "Che si può fare?"
Or "Lagrime mie"?*

She nods. *Those are gorgeous. Some of her best.*
She taps her fingers on the keys
and begins to play a version of "Che si può fare?"
I'm amazed at her ability to pull an idea
out of the air and turn it into music.

*Those are emotional songs.
You'd have to dig deep*, she says, and stops.
*But honestly, I think the expression of emotion
is why musicians exist.*

*We must channel all our experiences,
all our emotions, into each piece.
If we do not feel the tragedy, the lust, the love,
neither will our audience.*

I laugh out loud. *Well, that's a problem.
I haven't had that many experiences.
I've never been in a romantic relationship,
and Venice will be my first time out of the country.*

She puts her arm around me.
*There's so much to look forward to, Lula!
But for now you must learn to live in the world of dreams.
The world of your composer.*

*Your audience will be transported.
You are giving them a view through a keyhole—
into a world they have never known.*

It's pitch-dark and I'm tucked into bed

The door opens with a creak.
The bright light from the hallway assaults my eyes.
I squint.
Agatha! Where have you been?
I hear a crash and giggling.
Someone hisses, too loud to be a whisper.
Lula!

My heart stops beating. That's not Agatha.
Cass? I whisper,
and clutch my comforter around my breasts.
Lula! he says again,
this time so close to my face.
I'm afraid he can smell my sleep-breath.

What are you doing here? I hiss back.
I'm here too! Agatha giggles. They're both on the floor,
crawling like night-dwelling creatures of the deep.
We need you, Lula! Cass whispers,
and I brace myself.
Jesus. Please, God, tell me
they don't want to have a threesome.

We need you to sing for us, Agatha slurs,
her breath reeking of whiskey and weed.
They giggle again. Cass burps.
We have the best plan ever! they yell together.

Oh great. I close my eyes and breathe.
They're fucking wasted.

Agatha turns on the light and pulls me out of bed

Sit. She motions to a chair in front of the mirror.
Takes out her black liquid eyeliner and black lipstick.
Hell no, I say, pushing her hand away.
*This is not a movie where you turn me from a nerd
into a beautiful girl so I can get a boy.*

Agatha laughs and says,
*What do you think this is? The eighties?
No, girl. I understand your majestic power.
I'm just getting us ready for our costumes.*

I give her an evil stare. *Costumes?!*
She leans over to Cass and puts the eyeliner
and lipstick on him.
I'm slightly comforted by the gender equality,
until she pulls out three hazmat suits.
Silver plastic, with zippers running up the front.
And hoods.
We're going to wear these.

I look at the suit.
Please let me go back to bed.
Cass giggles and sways. He holds his hands out,
and belts in a fake announcer's voice,
*For one night! And one night only! Please join us in welcoming
RAGE AGAINST THE MINSTRELS!
Or maybe EARTH, WIND, AND SHIRE?
Or maybe CROSSBOWS & ROSES?
BLACK DEATH METAL?*
Okay. Okay. He shrugs. *We haven't found a name yet,
but whatever we call ourselves, we're going to be EPIC!*

I can't help but absorb his excitement
as they zip into their suits.
*My buddy at Berklee just texted.
They're having an open-mic night at ZuZu.*

He wants us to perform.
I look at my watch. It's already ten thirty.

We don't have a band—we haven't practiced.
Agatha rubs my back, which feels bizarre
since she's now wearing a medical suit specifically
designed to cut down on physical contact.

*We're going to play contemporary covers,
with our medieval instruments*, Agatha explains.
*You'll know the songs. And you're a pro.
And we don't have to be perfect. It's just for fun.*

Music? Just for fun?
Music is pain, and practice, and self-doubt.

Just as I'm about to protest,
she whips out a desk-sized Autoharp
and starts to play "Zombie" by the Cranberries.
Where has she been keeping that thing?
Under her bed? She sounds like a fairy bard.
I laugh at her hammered focus.
Seriously, hammered.

I feel too tired to argue.
What's with these ridiculous outfits?
Agatha puts down the harp and zips me into the suit.
Aren't they fabulous?!
Plus, they're the only costume that had sizes to fit us all.
She pulls up the hood. I pout. Cass laughs.

Okay. I'll sing for you, but you have to pick songs I know.
Cass jumps up and gives me several badly aimed high fives.
You won't regret this, I promise!

He shoots his fist into the air and yells,
For one night only . . .
EXCALIBUR ROCKS!

To my surprise

Cynthe is waiting outside the residence hall,
wearing the hazmat suit, black eyeliner,
and black lipstick. She's got a wooden flute
in one hand and a tambourine under her arm.

I give Cass a side-eye and whisper,
Who invited Praying Mantis?

He pats me on the back.
Cynthe's not that bad once you get to know her.
She has a good time every now and then.
And she looks so cute in her costume!
he adds, and blows her a kiss.

Cynthe scowls at him.

I'd hit that, Agatha says, and spanks her butt.

Cynthe takes a swig from a flask
and tucks it into her mirrored Doc Martens,
and says matter-of-factly,
Looks like you already did.

We walk a few blocks

to the Downtown Crossing stop
and ride the Red Line to Central Square.

We climb the stairs to the street.
A gust of cold air hits us, and the hazmat suits stiffen.
Cars are honking, taxi drivers yelling.
Exhaust spits from tailpipes.
It smells like piss.

I've been coming here since I was a kid,
but the pandemic years
made this place pretty rough.
Junkies swarm the bus stop next to the pharmacy.
A woman barfs into the bushes.

A man with rotten teeth,
and a broken cigarette hanging out of his mouth,
weaves right and left,
and fixes us with an angry stare.

You lost, or something? he murmurs under his breath.

His friend puts him in a headlock.
Forgive my pal here.

He looks at our silver suits and releases a low whistle.
Nice uniforms, space cadets.

He flashes a small plastic baggie
in front of my face.
It's filled with shards of ice.
Yah wanna fly to the moon?

I shake my head,
hold the back of my hand to my nose,
and keep walking.

ZuZu restaurant

is warm and inviting,
and smells like peppers and onions and za'atar.

I breathe deeply,
and my mouth begins to water.

Several groups are crowded onto wooden benches,
leaning over plates of pita and hummus,
trying to talk over the beat of the bass
and the drums pounding
through the floorboards below.

We pay a five-dollar cover and head downstairs to the stage.
I'm freaked that the bouncer might ask for ID,
but he sees our costumes and musical instruments
and waves us in.

*There's a rumor they're going to tear this place down
to build a six-story hotel,* Cass whispers, and frowns.
*This is where the Flaming Lips, Public Enemy,
Modest Mouse, and Elliott Smith got their start.*
He shrugs and smiles.
*Artists always lose when there's money to be made.
I guess we chose the wrong profession.*

The room is packed with college kids
holding red Solo cups filled to the brim with frothy beer.
Boston bros with backward baseball hats
and polo shirts and deck shoes.

One says, *Oh shit, bruh!* He laughs into his hand
as he gestures to our crew.

Cynthe, with eyes as cold as a lady mantis,
holds her fingers in a V and shoots her
long pierced tongue in between. They stare,
open-mouthed, then look away, avoiding her.
Girl's got guts, I'll give her that much.

Cass shoulder-thump-hugs the guy at the side
of the stage with a clipboard.
He puts our name on the list.

Agatha comes back from the bar,
bobbing her head, shaking her shoulders to the music.
Three drinks in her hands.

She gives one to Cynthe and one to me.
I sip my beer slowly, knowing I have to sing.

Maybe it's the beer,
or Agatha's adorable dance moves,
but I don't feel nervous.

I've never sung at a bar, to this type of crowd.
I'm used to intellectuals and grandmas.

The band ahead of us has a rockin' drummer.
He's setting the beat so thick
that it's ringing in my ears and chest.
I feel giddy.

Finally it's our turn

Cass sets an iPad on a stand, so I have lyrics.
I press my lips to the microphone.
It smells like beer.

I test it with a trill of my voice, to see how hot it is.
Someone hoots from the audience.

Cass raises his eyebrows. He leans toward my ear
and whispers, *I think you're going to like this.*

His breath on my neck, my mouth pressed to the mic.
My chest flutters and my thighs grip.

He smells like citrus and soap,
and as soon as he pulls away, I miss him.

He's so beautiful
standing in the stage light.

Smiling a wide grin, shoulders back,
confident.

I glance at Agatha,
worried she's seen our connection.
She has claim on Cass,
and I don't want to mess that up.

She's sitting on a stool, beaming,
hugging her Autoharp,
like goddamn June Carter.

Cynthe wets her whistle between her lips.

With one breath out

Cass and Agatha begin to play, lute and harp
weaving in and out, dancing together.
Sweet, yet dissonant.
Cynthe breathes into the whistle,
pumping her boots against the stage to keep time.

I ring in, high and clear,
medieval-ized lyrics to the song "Creep" by Radiohead.
The audience slowly stops milling around.
They are poised with glasses to their lips.
They've never heard anything like this.
They don't know what to make of it.
They're captivated by us. Futuristic beings,
playing songs they know,
with instruments they don't recognize.

My voice floats
through the room like a feather.
I make them believe it
when I tell them—I want a perfect body.
I want a perfect soul.

We move on to a medieval version of
"Holding Out for a Hero" by Bonnie Tyler.
My voice high and classical, I raise my hands and plead,
Whither have the heroes gone? Oh, where is fair Gawain?
Where is gallant Galahad to take the bridle rein?
When I approach the chorus, my voice builds.
I see the audience's expressions,
and laughter bubbles in my throat.
I need a hero. I shall hold out for a hero till
the morning light! He must be assured. E'er true to his word.
With a wit that will thrill and excite.
Thrill and excite!

I point to Cass. He jams out on his lute,
while I cascade notes over the top.
I dance around the stage,
swinging my hair,
pumping my legs up and down,
thinking of the tractor-racing scene
in the movie *Footloose*.

The audience is getting into it now,
the fast tempo,
the urgency of my voice.

We end with "Bad Romance" by Lady Gaga,
and they go crazy, throwing themselves
into a twirling mosh pit of bodies.

We bow together and jump off the stage.
Cass lifts me far off the floor in his long arms.
TALLULAAAAAAH! That was AMAZING!
I breath in his citrus smell. Feel his lean muscles.
He squeezes me. I come back to my body
when he plonks my feet back to the earth.

I turn to Cynthe and Agatha, trying to draw attention away
from my flushed cheeks, and say, *You sounded so good!*
Agatha hugs me. *OH MY GOD! We could not have done it
without you! You sing like a freakin' angel!*

We walk upstairs, and one of the frat boys runs up to us.
*Dudes! You know you're low when you're crying in a bar
to a medieval rendition of Radiohead,
but seriously, that shit was deep!*
The guy gives me a fist bump.
You got a hell of a voice, sister.

Cass looks at me and says,
I told you this would work! Just wait until Venice!

Cass grabs four kebabs

wrapped to go,
and we eat them walking down
a sidewalk lit by streetlights.
I inhale the pita with chicken,
warm onions, red peppers,
garlic, and yogurt.
Nothing has ever tasted so good.
The pulse of the stage
still coursing through my blood.
Surrounded by friends.

I crumple my kebab wrapper

walk across the street to toss the garbage into a trash can.

I see the man with rotten teeth staring at us.

He throws his beer bottle hard against the cement
and runs toward me.

I hear glass shattering.
ALIEN!

He screams, and he reaches out,
grabbing me around the throat.

No. I shake my head. *It's just a costume!*
The words are lost.

He shoves me against the alleyway,
presses his palm hard on my windpipe.
I try to shake my head.

No.
He tightens his grip.
Help. No. Help.
I can't talk. I can't breathe.

I see Cass run.
I hear Agatha scream.
Cynthe is calling someone.
Please call the police. Please.

I HATE YOU AND YOUR ALIEN FRIENDS!
The man is screaming, spitting words into my face.
I can see the foam on his lips.

Cass is talking calmly.
Desperately trying to pry the man's hands from my neck.

This is Lula. She's my friend.
This is a costume. She's not an alien.
You need to let her go. Right. Now.

I feel my blood pulsing into my eyes.
Tears fill my vision.

My ears are ringing. I can't hear Cass anymore.
I can't breathe. I can't speak. Help me. Help me.
I have no voice. I look at the man's blank eyes.
I'm going to die.

(CHORUS)

Fear:

touch the fragile

the hot

the sheltered

white fire

of destruction

go deep, into

the smoldering eye,

I see you

and love you

in your most

vulnerable place

7
Barbara

Venice, Italy
1635

What do you plan to do with that knife?

Ferrante sneers.

He motions to me
and turns to the men.

I, of course,
am open to the inclusion of women
in our circle.

We are an academy of bold thinkers.

But when the women arrive,
they bring their illogical
plans and passions
with them!

The room erupts in laughter.

I look down at the kitchen knife
I am holding like a weapon.

I came to cut the cake.

But I heard all the nonsense
you were spouting!

Ridiculous words!
I couldn't help myself!

Ferrante's smile widens.

Exactly the point
I believe
I was making.

You women
just can't control yourselves.

Stop it, Ferrante!
She's just an ordinary kitchen maid!
Leave her alone.

Nicolò takes a step closer.
I know he wants to help.

He sees that I am in pain.

He's right.
I am just an ordinary kitchen maid.

Ah! My dear Nicolò!

That is where you are wrong!
There is nothing ordinary about her!

My head whips around
so hard, my neck hurts.

Signor Strozzi walks to the doorway.
His shined high-heeled shoes
click with each step.

He takes my hand
and whispers,
Do not worry,
ragazza brillante.

He makes a grand gesture,
and bows to the crowd.

I am amazed that the wig he is wearing
stays on his head.

She is no common servant.

I hold my breath.
Yes. I am.
The most common.

Bastarda.

Signore drags a small wooden table
in front of me.

He motions for me to stand
on the tabletop.

Sing,
he whispers.

I look at him with shock.
I do not move a muscle.
Signore?

He calms me
with a hand on my shoulder.

I have heard you in the kitchen.

Sing for them,
as you sing for yourself.

I hesitate.
The room is filled
with noblemen.

Some,
the doge's Council of Ten,
who,
with a flick
of their wrists,
could send me
to prison for life.

Without reason.
Without a trial.

Show them
how foolish they are.

Signor Strozzi
smiles
in a way
that makes me believe.

I could have it all.

I reach

for signore's outstretched hand.

Step onto the table.

Tuck the knife
into the tied waist
of my apron.

Look
at the men
who are waiting
for a laugh.

I elongate my spine
until I am as tall
as I can be.

Place one hand on my stomach
and one on my heart.

I will not sing for them.
I will sing for me.

I close my eyes

and let my breath
fill me.

    Vi bacio e v'ascolto.

I kiss you and listen to you.

I keep my eyes shut.

My voice envelops
the room.

Full, warm, and round.

It swells against
the stone walls.

A slow moving
wave
that hits the mouth
of a cave
and fills it.

    Ma se godo un piacer,
    l'altro m'e tolto.

If I enjoy one pleasure,
the other is taken from me.

The wave
spills
into the ocean
again.

I engage my abdomen to make notes
cascade.

Droplets falling
into the sea.

Quiet.

Che soave armonia

What sweet harmony

I take one more
deep breath
and release it slowly
into the sweetness and strength.

O cari baci, o dolci detti

Oh dear kisses, oh sweet sayings

Crescendo.

Hold.

Open palms.
Arms held wide.

After I release my breath,
the sound
remains in the air.

Hovers.

Until it fades
to a humming silence.

My cheeks turn crimson

I crack my eyelids.

No one moves.
No one speaks.

I have no idea what to do.

Or where
to place my hands.

I open my eyes
all the way
and see stunned expressions,
mouths agape.

I look at the floor.

Don't cry.
Don't let them see you cry.

Brava!

Nicolò stands,
laughing with amazement.

He cups his hands
around his mouth and hoots again,
Brava!

Others join him.

Stand and shout,
Brava! Brava! Brava!

Seated and deadpan,
Loredano muses,

*How in the world
did a kitchen maid
learn a song
by Maestro Monteverdi?*

He continues,
A simple madrigal.

*Clearly not one
of his more complicated pieces,
to be sure.*

*But still, I want to know,
where did you learn it?*

Signor Strozzi
implores me
with his raised eyebrows
to answer Loredano.

Before I admit
that I have spent
my entire childhood
eavesdropping
through a keyhole
in the door,
Nicolò defends me.

*Who cares where she learned it!
She is magnificent!*

Others join in
with more applause.

*Can you imagine
if she were
to receive proper training?*

And learned to play the theorbo?

*She would transform into Flora
before our very eyes!*

Ferrante snorts.
*Can you imagine a servant
receiving music lessons
like a gentleman?*

He laughs again for effect.
How absurd!

*We would be better off sending her
to l'ospedale
to join the other abandoned
forlorn girls
and their violins!*

*Or to Madame Carmina
to become a courtesan.*

*Then she could really learn
how to move us!*

One of the men hollers
from the back of the room.

*What about her mother, Isabella?
La Greghetta!*

*She really knows her way
around a flute!*

The crowd erupts in laughter.

Signore looks
like he's going to hit someone.

Nicolò stands and shouts,
*Give her lessons!
She deserves it!
She is a siren!*

Another chimes in,
The gods have blessed her with natural talent!

Ferrante stands
and points at Strozzi.
*I'd bet you
one hundred ducats
that your servant cannot learn
the art,
the technique,
the seduction . . .*

He pauses for effect.

The glorious craft of music.

Loredano,
will you hold an event
at Palazzo Ruzzini?

The crowd hushes.

Loredano
looks lazily up from his drink.

How could I say no to academic inquiry?
To the testing of a hypothesis?

It seems only appropriate
to give my humble abode—
in the name of science.

The men cheer.

Ferrante hushes the crowd and adds,

That is,
only if she has the balls
to stand in front of us again!

Oh wait, I forgot!

She doesn't!

The men hoot and holler.

A nobleman in the back shouts,
How can you be so sure?

Laughter erupts once more.
Signor Strozzi starts pacing.

What are you saying, Ferrante?
Are you proposing a wager?
You know I am a betting man!

He begins to dance,
waving his arms,
while others cheer him on.

How will we know if I have won?

Signore looks around the room,
asking for suggestions.

Nicolò walks to me.
His olive-green eyes
sparkle
as he takes my hand
in his.

He presses his lips
against my skin
and then holds my palm
to his cheek.

My stomach flutters
from his warmth.

She will make men cry
with her beauty
and her brilliance.

Strozzi hops on one foot.

Indeed!
For what better way to prove
the truth of art
than by the emotions it demands?

If we cannot hide our tears,
we will know!

He turns to the men.

Agreed!

If she transforms herself,
and brings us to tears,
Ferrante will give me
one hundred ducats.

And his pride!

The men nod their heads
and laugh
in approval.

Strozzi slides
to Ferrante and Loredano,
and extends his hand.

May the best man win!

Their words echo in my ears

May the best man win.

What will happen
to the girl
who sings for them?

After they have
their fun.

ACT 2

(CHORUS)

Time:

You think you know me.

You do not.

You think I am linear.

I am not.

You think I can be calculated, controlled.

I cannot.

You think you remember everything.

You do not.

You think there is a beginning, a middle, an end?

It's all in your head.

I am a shattered mirror.

A rip, a scar

that cannot mend.

8

Lula

**Mount Auburn Hospital
Cambridge, Massachusetts
2025**

I hear the beeping before I open my eyes

A heart monitor tells me I'm alive.
Muted voices, whispering around me,
someone holding my hand.

I can't swallow. My throat is on fire.
I'm coughing. Nothing is coming out.
Hot daggers dig into my flesh. I can't breathe.
I open my eyes, and I see a hospital room
swirling around me.

My mother comes into focus.

*Lula, I'm here. I'm here. Everything's going to be okay.
You're okay.* I can hear the worry in her voice.
She's been crying. How long have I been here?
How long have I been asleep? I try to talk. I can't.
I reach for my mouth and feel a tube,
ice packed around my throat. *Don't talk, baby.
It's okay. Just rest. I'll call the doctor. Everything's okay.*

She leaves and returns with a team in scrubs
and white coats. I feel a snake being pulled
from my throat. I'm gagging, vomiting up plastic
from inside.

Lula has sustained a laryngeal trauma.
The good news is that we see no carotid intimal tears.
No rupturing. We see no spinal injury.
No fractures to the cartilage.

My mom digests the doctor's words,
and asks with a quiet voice,
Will she be able to sing again?

The doctor places her hand on my mom's shoulder.
Don't worry, Mama.
She will sing again.
There's no permanent damage.

The doctor writes a few notes.
She just needs ice, ibuprofen, and rest.

She hands me my release papers.
You're lucky, Lula.
You're going to be okay, she says to me
as she closes the curtain around us.

Mom lays her head on the bed.
I can hear her crying.

I'll take you home.
We can do a temporary withdrawal from school.
It will be okay.
Tears drip down her cheeks.

No, Mom, I croak.
I touch my neck, trying to understand the pain.
I struggle to say the words
I'm not going home.

She looks at the ceiling, as if praying for guidance.
Lula, you need time to heal.
We need you to get your voice back.
We can't lose this opportunity.

I squeeze her hand. I need her to listen to me.
She never listens to me.
You heard the doc. There's nothing wrong.
I need to get ready for Venice.
My mom looks at me sideways, like I'm singing off-key.
What are you talking about, Lula? Venice?

There's too much to say.
I feel too tired.
How can I convince her to let me go?
I've been chosen. To be part of an ensemble.
To compete in a music festival in Venice.
I swallow, hard and dry.
Motion for water. She hands it to me.
Over fall break. It's paid for.

She looks at me, wide-eyed.
Opens her mouth, but words don't come out.
Then she says,
You've only been at school a couple of weeks,
and you were chosen for this?

My hand around my throat. Burning fire.
Rasping. *I can do this, Mom.*

Oh, Lula. You can barely talk.
My mom shakes her head.

Out of the corner of my eye

I see Cass and Agatha and Cynthe waiting by the door.
They're here. They came.

Mom waves them into the room and then leaves.

Agatha hands me a fistful of wilted branches, goldenrod,
and asters that look like they came from an abandoned parking lot.
I picked them on the way here. She smiles. I smile back.

Cass sits by the bed and takes my hand.
We were so worried about you, Tallulah.
I half smile and wheeze, *I like to end a show with a bang.*
He laughs. *Well, you certainly ended this show . . .
more . . . banged-up.*

Cynthe stands in the corner. Her body poised in still-motion.
Staring into the hospital hallway.
Thanks for coming, Cynthe. I cough as the words scrape my throat.
She looks at her boots. *I had nothing better to do.*

I look at Agatha, and she rolls her eyes and whispers,
She asked to come. Cass squeezes my hand.
When do you get to come home?

The next day

my mom takes me back to campus.
She calls Professor Jenkins and tells her
I can attend class in a few days,
but I need to rest my voice.
Doctor's orders.

She tucks me into bed
with tea, blankets, magazines, candy,
and a snuggly bear.
She sits on the end, touching my feet.

Lula?
Yes, Mom?

I want to give you something.

She pulls the ring off her finger.
It's gold and contains a round red stone
carved with the symbol of three crescent moons
and a heart in the center.
She's worn this ring
for as long as I can remember.

I was so scared when you were born.
I had no idea how I was going to support you.
How I was going to be a single mom.
I was so young.

You know this story.

Your father never wanted to be a father.
He disappeared after high school.

I never saw him again.

It was just you and me, Lula-belle.

She wipes the tears from her eyes and pats my hand.

I felt so broken. My body and my spirit.
I felt so much shame.

I take her hand and hold it.

When I came out of the hospital, my mother gave me this.
She said it had been in her family for generations.
It's a ring for healing.

She places the ring on my finger,
and holds my hand again.

When you started singing,
I knew you had been born for a reason.

All of this pain, and sorrow, and struggle.
It was so you could have a chance.
A real chance.

I want you to have it all.
You're so special, Lula.

She wipes my tears away.
Pulls the blanket around me.
Tight and warm.

You've got to get healthy,
so you can go to Venice.

I jump out of bed and hug her.
She stands and hugs me back.
Tight.

*Call me every other day. I mean it.
I've been trying to give you space,
but now I need to know you're all right.*

*And if you don't get better in the next few days,
you're coming home.*

She points at her chest.
To me.

She walks to the door, and closes it behind her
with a click.

Agatha examines the ring

Whoa. Nice family jewels.
She turns my hand back and forth to admire the stone.
It's the symbol for the triple goddess.

Of course. She knows what it is.

What? I ask.
The triple goddess, she says.
And adds, *You know, maiden, mother, crone.*
There is a version of the triple goddess in many cultures.
Mediterranean, Celtic, Nordic.

The stone and the carving are really pretty.

She sits on my bed and pets my hair.
I've gotten more used to her need for physical touch.
It's starting to feel nice.

I'm so glad you're back, she says.
Me too, I say, and I mean it.

There's a knock on the door.
Cass sticks his head into the room.

Thought you might want some food.
He's holding a packed plate from the dining hall,
and sets it on my desk.

Thanks, Cass, I wheeze.
I stand up to hug him.

He embraces me, so gently,
I want to cry.

I wish I could live here.
In his safe, strong arms.

8
Barbara

Venice, Italy
1635

We must transform everything!

Signor Strozzi
and my mother

circle around me,
inspecting

my nest of curly black hair,
my teeth,
my callused hands and feet,
my breasts.

Stop!
I swipe their hands away.

> *You must be unrecognizable.*
>
> *Your clothes*
> *Your manners*
> *Your education*
> *Your hair*
> *Your smell*

What's wrong with my smell?

> *We will create a woman of opulence.*
> *A woman to be desired.*

I like the way I am!

> *Ragazza brillante!*
> *Of course!*
> *You know I adore you.*

My mother hugs me
and smooths my hair.

> *My love, we are trying*
> *to help you.*

A sinking feeling
hits my stomach.

I feel like I will vomit.

My mother
touches
my cheek
and breathes,
Shhhhhhhh.

She's trying
to calm
a skittish beast.

I am the beast.

> *We want them to see what we see.*
> *The beauty, the fire inside you.*
> *You don't have to hide it anymore.*

Who will own this fire?
After I am . . .
transformed.

I run the list of options in my mind.

The prison.
L'ospedale.
The convent.
A husband.

The many men
of the academy.

Signor Strozzi
gives me a weak smile.

> *In two months' time,*
> *on the eve of your sixteenth birthday,*
> *we must create an illusion*
> *that you are*
> *a grand dame of music!*
>
> *They must be completely*
> *transfixed*
> *by your charms.*

My mother hugs me again,
with a melancholy
that breaks
my heart.

For her,
and for me.

> *After that,*
> *we can talk about where a girl,*
> *a woman, like you*
> *belongs.*

Being trained to be a lady

has its advantages.

Signor Strozzi leads me
to a long table
in the dining room.

He motions for me
and my mother
to sit at one end.

He sits at the other end.

A vast space between us.

> *You must learn how to eat.*

I know how to eat.

> *You must learn to eat . . .*
> *not like a peasant.*

He chuckles
and adjusts his wig.

> *You must remember,*
> *Rossini and Mancini*
> *are here to serve you.*

Rossini snorts.

> *First,*
> *place your napkin on your lap.*

> *They will approach you with a bottle*
> *to fill your glass.*

*Then they will place
the primo piatto,
the first course,
in front of you.*

Mancini fills a tall flute
with prosecco,
and I reach for it.

*Per l'amor di Dio!
For God's sake!
Keep your hands in your lap!*

*You are here to be served!
Let them serve you!*

Mancini places the glass on the table.
*Here you are,
Your Royal Highness.*

Rossini serves me a plate
of linguini with clams.

The shells have fallen open,
exposing the soft
animal inside.

Signor Strozzi
uses a fork
to roll the linguini,
then shovels the noodles
into his mouth
and licks the oil
from his mustache.

Now you can eat!

I give
Rossini
a slow, wicked
smirk,
and place
the first bite
in my mouth.

The taste of oil and garlic
and seawater
linger on my tongue.

I really do feel
like a princess.

They take me to a dress shop

The tailor pulls out bolts
of silk damask.

One is the color
of cherries
ripening in the sun,
another as green
as the forest floor.

Tyrian purple.
The color of royalty.

Cerulean, the water
that surrounds our island.

Blue and green
sparkling like a gem.

Silver flowers
and gold leaves
intertwined.

A goddess's garden.

I run my hand
over the table covered
in rolls of fabric,
straight from the loom.

Each one cut
with silk velvet
designs
that caress my hand
as it glides.

The tailor turns his nose up
at my mother.

Nonetheless
he guides me to a mirrored glass,
holds the fabric
to my face
to see which color
makes my olive skin glow.

My mother speaks.

> *We will need enough*
> *for one evening dress.*
>
> *Also, draped curtains for two windows,*
> *bedding,*
> *and one table covering*
> *for her room.*

My body snaps
toward my mother.
My room?

I'm going to have a room?

My own room?

> For now.
> Signore wants you
> to have space to practice.

And where will you sleep?

> I think you know
> where I sleep most nights.

With that,
she gives me a wink
and turns to the tailor,
who gives her a sour look.

> And one dress
> for me
> made of this.

She points to a roll of midnight blue
cut with black velvet,
then turns to me.

> This color
> makes me think of the sky
> at the beginning
> of a storm.

> The kind of storm
> that no one knows is coming.

> But when it arrives,
> it makes
> even the strongest men
> take shelter.

9
Lula

New England Conservatory of Music
2025

Even though

the doctor has pronounced me healthy,
I can hardly move. I can hardly talk.

I have to return to class.

Agatha helps me put on clean clothes
and a scarf to hide the outline
of a purple thumb
and fingerprints on my neck.

We make tea with lemon
from a kettle in our room.
I wrap my palms around the warmth.

When Professor Jenkins sees me,
she encloses me in a hug.
She doesn't let go for a while.

Oh, Lula! I can't imagine! I'm so sorry!
She wipes tears from her eyes,
and I'm honestly touched to see
how much she cares.

I'm just glad to be here, I say, my voice still hoarse.
I hope I can get back to singing soon.

I take the seat between Agatha and Cass

directly across from Madison,
who has her legs draped over Brick.

What were you guys even doing in Central Square?
Busking? I bet your donation bucket was empty.

Next time you should bring your tambourine,
Brick suggests.
And pepper spray, Madison adds.

I make eye contact with Cynthe.
She's holding a bass drum mallet above Madison's head,
a look of rage in her eyes.

I want to say we formed a band
and played our first show at a packed club.
And guess what?
We Excalibur Rocked it.
It was so much fun,
and she wasn't invited.

I want her to feel excluded for once in her life.

Cass breaks in.
We were playing out at an open-mic night.
Trying something new.
We should get you and Lula on harmonies next time.

My stomach drops.

Madison curls her lips into a smile.
Ooooo! I would love to sing at an open-mic night with you guys!
Oh wait. I forgot. . . .
She looks at Brick and rolls her eyes.
I don't sing for free.

Okay! Let's focus!

We need to talk about logistics.
I can hear Professor Jenkins talking, but it sounds
like she's speaking through a distorted mic.

I was fine a moment ago. Now my ears are ringing.

It's going to be temperate weather,
potentially acqua alta, *which means "high water,"*
when the tides rise and water fills the streets.
It can be a bit disorienting, but it's usually safe.

Bring sweaters and raincoats,
but also be prepared for warm weather.
October is the most dazzling month in Venice!

I close my eyes. They won't focus.
My heart is beating fast. My chest is tight.

Madison, what are you thinking for your solo?
Madison stands and says,
"Maria, dolce Maria" by Francesca Caccini.
Jenkins nods in approval.
I like it! Another female composer.
That will complement Lula's piece by Barbara Strozzi.
She hesitates and looks at me with sadness.
That is . . . if she's feeling better.

My blood is pumping too hard.
I can feel it in my stomach.
I need to lie down. On the floor.

Has the ensemble chosen their piece?
She motions to Cass, Agatha, and Cynthe.

I feel my body swaying slightly.
I don't know if I can stay upright.

Agatha turns and looks at me.
She mouths, *Are you okay?*
I grimace.

She grabs my hand as if to cover up
what's happening. She starts talking loudly.
*There are so many amazing pieces by Handel and Bach
during that time. I think we're going to choose one of those.*
Cass nods. *I can get behind that.*

And, Brick? Jenkins asks.
Brick stands, mimicking Madison.
I have chosen quite a unique song.
He shifts his eyebrows up and down.
*I think you're all going to like it.
It's called "What Can We Poor Females Do?"
Madison and I can sing it, as a duet.*

Cynthe yells, *Are you kidding? No!*
Brick yells back, *Why not?*
Cynthe crosses her arms. *Because that is the WORST song.*
She slumps down in her chair.
*It should be titled
"What We Powerful Females SHOULD NOT Sing!"
It's obnoxious and sexist!*
She puffs her lips and closes her eyes.

Brick turns to Cass and says,
I think it's hilarious. Am I right?
Cass shakes his head vehemently and replies,
Don't bring me down with this sinking ship, bro.

I feel like I am on a ship.
Twisting, turning.
My stomach is about to empty onto the carpet.
Why are they still talking?

Okay! Jenkins says. *Let's keep thinking about Brick's song, but right now I want to tell you about our itinerary.*

We'll spend five days in Venice.
Tour many of the museums and tourist destinations,
see a show at La Fenice opera house,
and, of course, attend the performances of the festival.

I can't focus. I can't listen.
My eyes are blurring.
Professor Jenkins hands out a schedule of events.
A packing list.
Agatha takes my copies for me.

And we're staying at my favorite hotel in Cannaregio.
Jenkins claps her hands together.
It's going to be a dream!

Agatha holds my hand

as we leave the building.
She finds a bench for us to sit on.
I start to cry.
I don't understand.
If nothing is wrong with my body.
Why do I feel so awful?
She cradles me in the crook of her arm,
my head against her neck. I've never had a sister.
This is what it must feel like.
It's going to take a little while.
You're going to be okay.
I squeeze my eyes hard, trying to stop the tears.
I hope so.

It's time

My first vocal lesson since the attack.

Jenkins is waiting at the piano.
She rises to greet me.

I'm so glad you're here. Are you ready to begin?
Her smile is encouraging. I nod.
I take a sip of my tea with lemon.

Have you tried to sing on your own?
I shake my head.

She sits again at the piano,
and motions for me to join her.

Your mom told me your vocal cords are not damaged.
What a blessing.

Let's start slow. Don't be afraid.

Your voice may sound different.
It may take some getting used to.

Let's start with some gentle humming.

She starts the scale at a very comfortable spot
for my voice. The first notes are hesitant and cloudy,
but I can sing in this middle range.

There's no rush. We have time to experiment.
Just let it flow.

I gain confidence. I try to sing.

As we rise,
my voice hits the part of the scale
where usually the magic and glitter
and velvet come, the point when people
open their eyes wide
in awe because it sounds
like the inside of a shell, or a bell.

I cannot feel the resonance.
I cannot feel the shine.

A hand reaches around my neck and squeezes.
A knife severs the voice from my throat.

I can't

A wave of dizziness hits me. I can't.
My ears are ringing. I'm failing.
I won't make it.
My mother. My training.
The money. The time. My childhood.
A body I don't recognize.
I am a ghost, without a voice.
No one will love me if I can't perform.
I look at Professor Jenkins,
my hands around my throat.
She reaches out.
I shake my body. She cannot
help me. She cannot heal me.
I run.

Out of the office

through the carpeted hallways,
the lobby, the door, and into the night.
I run across the campus,
down the crowded sidewalks,
past honking cars, tires squeaking.
I stop.
Body bent to catch my breath,
straighten, wipe my tears away.
Stare at a pigeon pecking
a piece of pizza on the concrete.
Its purple-and-green slick collar
shining in the streetlamp's light.
Innocent eyes.
I want to take her home with me,
give her a nest and some seed.
She hops three times
off the sidewalk
onto the street, and she stands there,
head up, proud, looking at me.
Nature and concrete.
How pretty she looks. How majestic.
Her purple necklace,
white-striped wings, against
the black asphalt. The subway
rumbles under the walk and hisses
steam from the grates.
The light turns green,
gas and engines rev, cars advance
at a breakneck speed.
The pigeon, still staring at me,
smashed,
in one simple rotation
under the weight of a wheel.
Iridescent feathers, gray down,
and blood explode in silence
as the cars keep honking

and the people keep eating their pizza,
and I cry alone on the sidewalk,
wishing I could leave
this city, where everything real
and colorful and alive
is crushed.

(CHORUS)

Bells:

We know

how difficult it is

to wait

alone

high in a tower

wondering

when we will ring

again

9
Barbara

Venice, Italy
1635

Today is my first lesson

with Francesco Cavalli,
one of the most famous musicians
in all of Venice.

He sings
at the Basilica di San Marco
with Maestro Monteverdi,
the father of opera.

There are rumors
that Cavalli is working
on an opera of his own.

What will he think of me?
A servant,
in a holy place of music.

I touch the covering on my hair,
my simple linen dress,
the coffee-stained apron.

Inhale. Exhale.

I must go to my first lesson,
just as I am.

Common. Humble.
Ready to learn.

Someone is knocking

I run to answer it,
afraid this will make me late
for my lesson.

Nicolò is standing
at the door.

I scowl at him.
Why are you here?

    Buongiorno, signorina.

He takes the
feathered cap from his head.

It matches
the quilted green
velvet vest,
which accents his
olive-green eyes.

    I'm here to escort you.

Where?

    To your lesson with Cavalli.

Does Signor Strozzi know you are here?

    Sì, va bene.

    He asked me to come.

I don't move from the stoop.
I'm not sure what to do.

This is my first time walking
alone with a man,
through the streets.

What will people think?

A man of nobility,
with a young female servant.

Heads will swivel.

> *Come, signorina.*
> *Let's walk together.*

He bows,
as if dancing.

He takes my hand,
like I'm a *donna,*
a noblewoman.

Holds it against his lips.

He looks up at me
and smiles.

Then straightens
and becomes serious.

> *I won't let anything*
> *happen to you.*

I snort.

I can take care of myself.

I've never had an escort before.
I've always been fine.

Except with Ferrante!
And Loredano!

And YOU!

I point a finger in his face.

> *I'm sorry.*
> *I should have done more . . .*
> *to stop Ferrante.*
>
> *Please, don't be angry with me.*

Servants don't need escorts.

> *I know, but now*
> *it's different.*

Why?

> *It just is.*

I close the door behind me.

We walk in silence
side by side.

Anger
smoldering
in my chest
as we wind our way
though the dark, narrow
alleyways.

Nicolò sneaks shy glances

Tries to make small talk.

He asks me
about my mother,
my favorite foods,
if I have siblings,
and then the uncomfortable silence
returns.

Begrudgingly,
I ask him a question.

Are you originally from Venice?

He sighs with relief.

> *I was born around Verona,*
> *but I came to Venice to study music.*
>
> *I've been composing.*
>
> *I'm working on*
> *a triple-time bel canto,*
> *and I want to learn*
> *to write music*
> *for multiple voices.*
>
> *I'm not great yet,*
> *but I hope to be someday.*

I wish you could teach me,
I say, and then blush.

I want to hide
behind a rock,
in a shell,
under a shoe.

His face brightens.
He smiles.

> *I would love to teach you.*
> *Strozzi wants the best for you,*
> *and from his perspective,*
> *that's Cavalli.*
>
> *We're always competing,*
> *and unfortunately,*
> *Cavalli always wins.*
>
> *I suspect*
> *he doesn't even know*
> *we're competing,*
> *but I do.*

Nicolò chuckles at his own joke.

I laugh with him.

He's softer without
Ferrante and Loredano.

Shy and friendly,
warm.

No.

He's rich and entitled,
I think.

He has no idea
what it's like to be me.

Trapped.
Illegitimate.
No hope for the future.

He's a man.

A man
who postulates,
and drinks grappa,
and stands
in front of a crowd
and says that women
are not passionate enough
to create music.

I close my heart to him.

Even though
his green eyes twinkle
when he smiles.

Cavalli is surprisingly young

and quiet.

His shoulders are slumped.

Hair hidden
under a monk's cap.

A pointed beard
and mustache
make him look like a boy
masquerading
as a man.

Nicolò introduces us,
then excuses himself.

Cavalli motions for me to take a seat.

>   *Welcome,*

he whispers,
and hands me a lute.

I press its round body
against my stomach.

Run my fingers
over the smooth surface of
the neck, the strings.

>   *Good.*

>   *You must get to know*
>   *each other.*

>   *Become friends.*

I smile,
but he does not.

He is serious,
without humor.

Filled with respect
for his art,
he wants me to feel
this too.

Cavalli picks up another lute
and sits next to me.

Plays one note,
and then motions for me
to do the same.

His note sounds rich and warm,
a songbird hovering,
pulsing against
the wind.

My note
sounds like a bald
baby bird.

   Again.

He plays the note
even louder
and fuller
than before.

   Use the full tip of your finger.

   Press harder.
   Feel the vibration.

I press the first finger
of my left hand
into the string,
and I pluck
the same string
with my right forefinger.

The sound shivers
and hums
across my body.

   Yes.

   This string is made
   from an animal.

   You can make it
   come alive again.

I pluck notes
one
after another.

He shows me how
to hold my hand,
like it's grasping
an apple.

The apple cannot
fall.

Learn
a simple chord.

My lips part.
My eyes narrow.
My chest heaves
with breath
and excitement.

I can make music.

Make an object sing
as strong
as a human voice.

I am not one body.
I am two.

Full of sound, and energy.

Harmony.

I feel
my heart
vibrating,
a plucked string.

I am the one
who has come alive.

Oh, Nicolò!

I exclaim
as he takes the lute case from me.

We exit the cathedral
and admire
the breathtaking view
of Piazza San Marco.

I open my arms,
close my eyes,
and breathe the salty air.

Twirl, in a circle,
so I can see every
magnificent building
and tower at once.

I want to tell him
everything.

*I have never in my life
experienced something so beautiful!
So real!*

*I have found the love of my life,
and it is a lute!*

Nicolò's shoulders
shake
with delight
as he sputters,
and grabs his chest.

    Ah! I am heartbroken!

I blush and giggle,
embarrassed,
but decide to play his game.

I place my hand
over my forehead
and act like a damsel
in distress.

*I am sorry, but I have
given my life to another.*

*An animal
that hungers
only for beauty.*

Nicolò pounds his chest.

*At least you have chosen
a lover I approve of.*

I'm just glad it's not Cavalli.

*We all know I can't compete
with that devil.*

No.
Not Cavalli!

*Although, I would love to learn
the art of love
from him.*

Nicolò gasps
and grabs my hands
in feigned shock.

I shake my head
and raise my brows.
The love of music.

Oh, thank God!

His hands are still holding mine.
We are smiling.

I feel his laughter.
The sway of his body.

The hum of the music
is still in me.

I tell my body to stop wanting

This man
is not for me.

It refuses.

My body betrays me.

Cheek.
Neck.
Breast.

I am red with heat.

He breaks away

Releases his hands.

Looks ashamed.

> *I need to take you home.*
> *They'll be worried.*

We walk without speaking.

Boots hitting
the cobblestones.

A fist beating
against
a closed door.

(CHORUS)

Time:

is a room

full of clocks

incessant ticking

each rotating gear

the pendulum swings

a moon and sun

the spinning plate

earth

the golden numbers

an arrow

spinning, spinning

all the clocks

ticking, ticking

never perfect

never perfectly

in sync

but not

far apart.

10

Lula

New England Conservatory of Music
2025

Session I

I am directed to a bland office, with a pothos plant
hanging at the top of the window, growing across the frame.
I sit on the blue couch across from an empty armchair.
A clock ticks on the wall.
A woman knocks and enters.

Luciana Garboni?
I nod.
I'm Patience. I'm a psychotherapist.
Your doctor has told me about your assault.
I've been waiting for you to come visit me.
I'm glad you finally did. I nod again.

Do you want to tell me what happened to you?
I shake my head. I can't tell the story again.

Do you want to tell me why you're here?
I open my mouth. Nothing comes out.

Session II

Do you feel like you're having lingering physical effects?
I look at her with piercing eyes, and say,
I can't sing.

She waits for me to say more.
The ticking of the clock, a metronome,
counting the beats of a song that will not end.

Finally she fills in the silence.

There are many things we can try.
Relaxation and focusing techniques.

Tapping therapy and EMDR
have been shown to be helpful when healing from trauma.

Even though the body may not be damaged,
it can retain memory of the trauma.
There can be anxiety, tension, and fear.

I wring my hands together.
Stare at the pothos plant that has twisted
and grown around itself.

Fear is the only emotion
that I can feel.

Session III

Sometimes trauma can bring up things from the past.
This compounded trauma can make us feel unsafe.

I look up to keep the tears from flowing down my cheeks.
I dig my thumbnail into my finger.

I close my eyes and try
to sink into the faux leather sofa,
try to disperse into the air like sound.

We need to try to find people and places, rituals
that make us feel safe and loved.

How do you do that? I want to say.
When my voice was what made me feel loved?
Close to my mom.
It was the one thing we shared.

I think about the years during the pandemic.
She wouldn't let me go back to school.
She chose to homeschool me instead.
Wouldn't let me perform.
We became an island of two in a sea of sadness.
Without theater, without choirs and concerts,
without applause.

All I wanted was to go to the conservatory.
To be out in the world. To feel normal again.
This is who I am.
This is who I was meant to be.

Now that it's time to become who I truly am,
I've lost everything.

It was taken from me.

I'm staring at a bowl of vegetable soup

I just can't.
I'm failing. I'm failing. I'm failing.

We should go dancing, Cass says, and grabs my hand.
I snatch it away.
If you think I'm going to a club, you're insane.
I want to go back to the room.
Agatha puts her hand on my shoulder.
No one is rushing you, Lu.
We just want you to be used to going out before we get to Venice.

We walk back to our dorm room.
I collapse onto my bed and speak my fear.
What if Jenkins won't let me go to Venice?

Cass avoids the question.
Grabs a fedora hanging on Agatha's bedpost.
He places it on his head, slightly cocked to the side.
Raises his eyebrows.
If you cannot go dancing, dancing will come to you.

Cass connects to our Bluetooth speaker.
Types a song into Spotify, and Whitney Houston's
"I Wanna Dance with Somebody" starts blaring.
He Latin dances his way over to me.
Don't you want to dance, Tallulah?

I shake my head.
He motions to Agatha, and she jumps.
They start mouthing the words at each other.
Faces close and smiling. Jumping and stomping.
The comfort between them is enviable.
They are so close, so sweet.
He gathers her into his arms and kisses her cheeks.
She softens into him.

Agatha leans down and pulls me up.
Cass hugs us both.
They sway with me in their arms.
I mouth the words to the song into Cass's chest.
A whisper. I want to sing the lyrics high and loud,
but my body and my mind just won't let me
be free.

Even though I can't sing

I attend the ensemble rehearsals.
I watch Brick and Madison smile at each other
as their hands and voices wind together.

Watching them flirt is as pleasurable
as watching a trombone player
empty their spit chamber, but I must admit,
they sound good together.

They've decided to bench
"What Can We Poor Females Do?"
much to everyone's relief, and have chosen
Stölzel's "Bist du bei mir,"
"If you are with me,"
which is so heartbreakingly exquisite.

I imagine that I could love them both.

Cynthe accompanies them on the harpsichord.
As soon as they're done, Brick flashes me
a smolder, and my stomach churns.

Cass is masterful at the lute.
His timing and emphasis are perfect.
He's wearing a black tank top,
his broad shoulders and biceps pulsing
to the rhythm of the music.
He smiles with each movement.
He's so beautiful.

My chest and cheeks flush
when I realize I've been staring at him
a little too long.

Agatha is graceful at the harp.
Her long, blond waves fall down her back,
her eyes closed.
Transported to another time.

I follow along with the sheet music.
I hope to add my voice,
but I'm still listening and waiting.

That evening

Agatha sits by my bed and holds my hands.
I want you to come with me.

Where? I groan. *I'm so tired.*
I just want my bed.

Come with me, she says again.
It's a place I really love.

She pulls me to my feet and gives me a hug.
You can wear comfortable clothing.
You don't have to speak.
It will be good for you. And for me.

She pulls out a clean pair of sweatpants, a sweatshirt.
She brushes my greasy hair and puts it into a ponytail.

Her loving support makes me want to cry.
Okay, but I want to come back soon, I plead.
She nods, and says, *It's just a short walk.*

We step into the moonlight

I can hear the hum of the night.
Grasshoppers and crickets singing
their last song before the frost arrives.

We walk to another dorm on campus,
climb a flight of stairs,
and she knocks on a door.

A tall, willowy woman
with waist-length hair greets us.
She has tattoo sleeves on both arms.
Ancient, scrolling art, symbols
and swirling spirals.

Agatha! I'm so glad you're here!
She grabs my hand and looks at me
with sapphire-blue eyes.
And you must be Lula. Welcome.

She motions us into a dark room with a pink hue,
candles, and sparkling lights.
It's filled with women sitting in a circle
on the floor.

Welcome to our harvest ritual,
she says, and motions for us to join the circle.

I look at Agatha, and whisper,
Where the hell am I? Are we joining a cult?

She chuckles. *Just relax.*
It's a women's group.
We meet when the seasons change.
Tonight we're doing sound healing.

When everyone is settled, the women join hands.
Everyone closes their eyes.
The woman with sapphire eyes speaks.

The symbol of the autumnal equinox
is the double spiral.
It illustrates the in breath and out breath,
the point of balance between the worlds,
the inner and outer journey.

Three women lift up large crystal bowls.
They tap them with wooden mallets.

A clear note,
then a vibrating resonance,
another corresponding note,
an echo.
The sound builds and builds
until my skull
feels like it's reverberating
with light.

This is the time of year when we release
what is not serving us.
Let it wilt to the ground.
Let it be buried.

Two other women add their voices,
singing with the cascading tonal notes.

And we dream of what we will plant.
What we want to grow.

One of the women cups her fingers.
The goddess within
holds all life in the palm of her hands.
She is always with us.

Agatha places one hand on the small of my back,
and the other women join her.
Each placing a hand on my arms,
shoulders, and back.

I don't mind their touch.
I feel comforted.
Held by this community.

They tap the crystal bowls again.

I close my eyes and imagine
a spiral, a labyrinth,
women connected.

A mirror of light, waves,
and sound.

10

Barbara

Venice, Italy
1635

My mother hands me a large box

tied with a velvet ribbon.

> *We thought you could use this.*
> *For your music lessons.*
>
> *While we wait for the performance gown.*

I open the lid
and peel back the crepe paper.

It's a dress
made from thin wool.

A deep reddish purple,
a blooming iris,
a newly ripened berry.

> *I thought the color would suit you.*
>
> *Contrast and brighten*
> *your dark hair, and skin.*
>
> *It's a practical dress for every day.*
>
> *When you go out,*
> *the town will think*
> *you've got someplace*
> *important to be.*

And they won't be wrong!

She kisses my forehead,
and I can tell
she is proud of me.

Tears fill my eyes.

*I won't let you down,
Mamma.*

> *You never could.
> I am always proud of you.*

She helps me into
this new dress.

It fits perfectly,
because of the tailor's careful
measurements.

She drapes
a white lace collar
around my neck.
Ties it and tucks it
into the bodice.

And secures
a matching, hooded cape
around my shoulders.

> *Now you are ready
> for a new life.*

I look at myself in the mirror.

I will wear this dress
as I learn and grow.

Into a woman.

A woman of promise.
A woman of intellect.
A woman of passion.

The woman
I know we both
want me to become.

I let down my hair

For the first time
since my childhood,
I will go outside
without a scarf tied
around my curls.

A sign
that I am no longer
a servant.

I sit in a chair
as my mother brushes my hair
and weaves purple ribbons
into the two braids
by my temples.
The rest of my hair flows
past my shoulders.

She holds up
a handheld mirror.

I barely recognize myself.

Hair flowing
like Botticelli's Venus.

A shimmering pearl,
emerging from the center of a shell.

I put down the mirror,
press my head
to my mother's stomach.
She leans to kiss me.

If I am no longer a servant,
what am I?

All I know

is that I want to play music
and sing.

Learn more.

Get lost
in the chapel.

Of myself.

A forest of
sound,
vibration,
pleasure.

I want to awaken
the animal,
let it roam
in the dark woods.

Instinct
and nature
alive

in my body,
my heart,
and my mind.

I wait on the steps for Nicolò

My borrowed lute in hand.

The crisp light
casts early morning shadows
across the windows
and eaves.

The sharp wind
twirls
my hair
and the edges
of my wool cape.

I see him
walking, distracted.

He's looking at the paper in his hand.

I wonder
if it's a new composition.

Nicolò, I shout.

He raises his head from his work.

Mouth opened
eyebrows raised
in genuine surprise,
he trips.

Body juts forward,
hands flail.
He catches himself
on the side of the building
next to the palazzo.

Sheepish and flustered,
he smooths his hair,
stuffs the paper
into his jacket,
and steps forward.

Barbara . . .

Hello, Nicolò.

You look . . .

Unable to complete the sentence,
he tries again.

Your hair . . .

I know. It's different.

Your dress . . .

My mother ordered it.

I smooth the skirt.

Wait
while he tries
to form a sentence.

Do I look ridiculous?

Am I trying to be something,
or someone,
that I can never be?

You . . .

What, Nicolò?
What?

He steps closer.

He touches my arm.

I can't breathe.

> *You are beautiful.*

His voice is thick
with emotion,
but he laughs it off.

> *I can't walk.*
> *Apparently I can't talk.*

> *I can't stop looking at you.*

His hand
feels warm,
solid and strong.

I do not
push him away.

A stranger passes

Buongiorno, he says,
and gives us a hard stare,
and keeps walking.

Nicolò jumps back,

> *We're late.*
> *We have to hurry.*

He walks ahead of me,
placing a large distance
between us.

Leaving me
aching,
wondering if I will ever
feel his warmth
again.

My brain feels soft

like a jellyfish
washed onto the shore.

Exposed.

I can't complete a thought.

Do I want him?
Do I hate him?

11

Lula

New England Conservatory of Music
2025

My phone rings

Agatha looks at me. *Expecting anyone?*
I shake my head and look at the screen.
It's Professor Jenkins.

Panic.

I tap the green button. *Hello?*

Hi, Lula. Thanks for picking up the call.
I just wanted to see how you're doing.

I'm good. . . .
I look at Agatha with wide eyes.
I press the speakerphone button
so Agatha can hear what's happening.

What the hell do I say?

I've been listening to Barbara Strozzi's opuses,
I mumble. *She's incredible. Her music sounds so modern.*
It's bizarre. And touching and spiritual.
Dark and beautiful.
It feels different from the other music of her time.
She was the original female singer-songwriter.
A seventeenth-century Taylor Swift.

Please don't pull me from the trip.
Please don't.

Jenkins breathes in and exhales.
I'm excited for you.
You seem to have found a perfect subject.

I feel connected to her,
I whisper.

Please don't cut me.
I can do it.
I think I can do it.
I'll get my voice back.
I swear. I think.
I want to promise.

Lula, I'm wondering how you're doing . . . emotionally.
Saliva sticks to my tongue, the inside of my cheeks.
I'm great! I croak.
I feel like I'm singing flat,
surrounded by a perfectly tuned choir.

I'm nothing. I'm dying inside.

Agatha sees that I'm sinking.
It's true, Professor Jenkins.
She's been getting outside. Sleeping and eating.
She's seeing a therapist.

Professor Jenkins pauses.
Is that you, Agatha?
She looks at me apologetically.
Yeah, I'm here too.

Great—I'm glad that Lula has you.
It sounds like you've been supporting her.

And, Lula, I'm proud of you for seeing someone.

I want to crawl under a piano bench.
Yes! Her name is Patience!
And she really is patient!
I say, with a little too much enthusiasm.
We're working together on coping mechanisms
and ways to experiment with my voice,
while I'm trying to sing again.

I grimace and close my eyes.
Please know how hard I'm trying.

Lula, I just want you to know
that even if you don't get your voice back,
we still want you to come on the trip.
But only if you feel . . . up for it.

I let out a huge sigh.
Thank you, Professor Jenkins.
I start to cry.

Oh, Lula.
I should have called earlier.
I didn't realize you were so worried.

The relief and comfort overwhelm me.
I promise I won't let you down.

Agatha puts her arm around me.

Jenkins continues,
Venice has a way of making people feel
more connected to their body and spirit.

I think it will be a wonderful time
for you to remember who you are.

You can still take in the history,
and think about Barbara
and what she would have experienced
living in the city in the sixteen hundreds.

This is half of the reason I designed this trip.
Our connection to history
can inform who we become as artists.

She pauses and shouts into the phone,
No *woman left behind!*

I call my mom before I start packing

Tell me if you need to come home.
Don't hesitate, okay?

I try to reassure her,
but I can barely control my own nerves.

I'll call you when I get back. I promise,
I say, trying to make my voice sound calm.

After I hang up,
I stuff black pants, tank tops, black sweaters,
and solid black walking shoes into a duffel bag.
I want to be as anonymous as possible.
Get lost. Blend in.

Agatha takes a sideways look at my suitcase
and throws in a red scarf, a halter-top sundress,
and a pair of red sandals.
Just in case! she says, and pecks me on my cheek.
I roll my eyes, but don't fight it.

She fills her suitcase with her usual scarves and flowy dresses.
I imagine her floating through Venice with a trail of men
crawling on their knees, begging for a kiss,
while Cass holds his hands up.
She's taken, he'll say, and dip her, kissing her neck
as the orange sun sinks into the canal.

Lula?
I look up and see Agatha staring at me.
Dreaming about some Italian dude?
I flick the back of my hand at her shoulder.
No. What were you saying?

She folds another dress into her bag.
I was saying, we can't travel with my harp.
I feel nervous about borrowing one.
What if it doesn't feel right?
I meet her eyes.
Agatha is nervous too.
Have you ever played another harp? I ask.
She tightens and releases her shoulders.
Yes. But it still feels weird.
Like I'm cheating on my best girl, Harper Lee.

Also, have I told you I get seasick?
And I've heard that Venice . . . has a lot of boats.
I squeeze her tightly.
For the first time in our relationship,
I'm the calm one.

I remember our first day, and ask,
Do you need me? You know . . . to help you breathe?

She laughs, quoting my line back to me,
I can breathe just fine on my own.
The instant she tries to reassure me, her face falls,
and she looks worried again.

I reach out for her.
It's true, you are an expert breather, but a hug might help.

I fall asleep, I dream

Hair swirls around my face, bubbles rise to the surface,
lightning shocks the water above. I hear singing through the dark.
There, in the distance. Electrical crack.
Soaked pages torn from a book. The sand shifting. A star.
The moon rising over the water. A tree. A door.
The room I've been searching for.
Through the water, swimming toward me, a siren.

11
Barbara

**Venice, Italy
1635**

Cavalli claps his hands

    You have been practicing!

Happiness spreads across my face
as bright as the jewels
in the Pala d'Oro,
the high golden altar
that brightens
the basilica.

I have, I say
as I blush.

    Good!
    You are a clever girl!

Maestro Cavalli?

    Yes?

I know you have things you want me to learn.
Songs you wish for me to play.

    Yes, I am trying to build new skills
    every week.

*Mastering the notes,
sight-reading,
timing.*

*Would it be okay
if I made songs of my own?*

*Compose?
Your own songs?*

*I hear music,
in my mind,
as if it's floating in the air.*

I would love to try to play it.

I don't see why not.

*It usually takes years
before you are able
to compose,
but if you would like to experiment,
I see no harm.*

Play on!

I find Nicolò

in the back of the church.

Sitting in a pew,
leaning forward
with clasped hands.

His long dark hair
falls across his shoulders,
his bent brow.

He's praying.

He looks so peaceful,
so innocent.

I don't want to disturb him,
but I want him to see me.

Are you praying for something?
Or asking for forgiveness?

I say, and blush.

Thinking about the alley,
his hand touching me.

How my body
longed to receive him.

Maybe
I should be the one
praying.

I want to take you somewhere

Nicolò says
as he stands.

He heads to the opening
of the nave.

This time
he looks back
to see if I'm following him.

We walk to the campanile

The clock tower.

El paròn de casa,
the master of the house,
looms over
Piazza San Marco
and the doge's palace.

Watches
for approaching enemy ships.

A golden angel
perched on top
guides Venetians home.

Rings
to alert the citizens.

One bell
to start and end
the day,
two to call
the Council of Ten,
three
to warn the people
of an execution.

We enter

through the arched marble
portico.

Climb the spiral staircase.

I need to pause
several times
to catch my breath.
Hundreds of stairs,
the air thins.

Finally
we arrive at the top.

Pigeons perched
in the eaves
scatter as we approach.

I lean over the edge
and gasp.

I can see the canal
winding
through the red rooftops
all the way to the sea.

Nicolò says,

> This is my favorite place.

It's breathtaking.

I raise my face to the heavens,
and open my arms.

I feel like God!

> *Don't let the pope hear you say that!*

I cover my mouth
and laugh.

> *It certainly gives perspective.*

Indeed.

> *Galileo used this tower*
> *as an observatory to study the skies,*
> *and this is where he demonstrated*
> *his first telescope to the doge.*
>
> *Right here,*
> *where we are standing.*
>
> *Do you know,*
> *Galileo believes*
> *we are not the center*
> *of the universe?*

That must be difficult
for a nobleman
to understand.

Nicolò chuckles,
but then
his eyes
shine like the golden mosaics
as he says,

> *Yes, but I believe*
> *when we find love,*
> *we rotate our lives*
> *around another person.*

*Everyone
needs the warmth
of the sun.*

He stares at me,
with parted lips.

I feel his warmth
heating my skin.

I want him to touch
my arm again.

He breaks my trance,
and waves his hands in the air.

*Enough about love.
This is serious!*

*Galileo was investigated
by the Inquisition,
and found guilty of heresy,
and put under house arrest.*

His expression changes.

*Sometimes
I wonder if God even exists,
and if our souls are immortal.*

*But I am not allowed
to have these thoughts.*

He shakes his head.

*I must not rock the foundation
of the church,
of society.*

> The Jesuits are attacking students
> in Padua,
> where Galileo teaches.
>
> Beheading those who preach heresy.
>
> Those who wonder about
> the nature of the universe,
> and scientific reasoning.
>
> They are coming after artists.
>
> Musicians.
> Freethinkers.

He pauses.

I don't know what to say.

I want to touch his hand,
but I hesitate.

> Even in Venice,
> we live in a bubble separated from Rome,
> but danger still exists.
>
> The Council of Ten can persecute
> anyone they perceive as threatening.
>
> We cannot go against
> our doge.
>
> We must make alliances.
>
> We must all know our places.

I know my place.

I don't belong anywhere.

He looks at me with sorrowful eyes.

You will find your place.
You will make a life, with music.

I don't know if that's possible, Nicolò.

As a man, you can have
your own life.

Make your own choices.

All of my choices
were taken from me
when I was born a woman.

What happens
when I show up at Palazzo Ruzzini?

What if I succeed?

What if I sing,
and Signor Strozzi
wins his bet?

What then, Nicolò?

Do I return to being a servant?
Do I have a choice?

He looks away,
and I know he can't answer
my question.

I breathe deeply
and try to change the mood.

*Cavalli told me
that Galileo's father
made lutes.*

And Galileo, too.

*I wonder if he ever saw similarities
between musical notes
and the stars in the sky.*

Nicolò smiles.

    They both make us feel heaven.

*And earth.
I smile back.*

The softness returns
to Nicolò's eyes.

I like talking about science,
and politics,
and love.

My heart beats faster
as he moves closer to me.

Places his elbows
on the guardrail
and rests his chin
on his hands.
Gazes
at the city below.

    We are so small.

Yes, we are small.

*But we are also capable
of creating
great beauty.*

He stands straighter,
and reaches for my hand.

Especially you.

I look down, ashamed,
unable to look at him.

*I'm worried
I won't learn fast enough.
I won't be good enough.*

I'm not.

He stands behind me,
leans his lips
next to my ear.

I feel his breath.
Ice and heat.

He points
to our city below
and whispers,

*All of Venice
is waiting for you.*

12

Lula

Above the Atlantic Ocean
2025

Airplane

We lull ourselves into thinking
that flying thirty thousand feet above the ground
is something common, normal, rational.
When the engines fire up, the metal shell
begins to hum, the flaps open and close,
and I suck poisoned exhaust into my nostrils.
I'm not so sure this is the best idea.
We jet across the runway,
backs plastered to our seats.
This is not safe. This is not wise.
Panic spreads through my chest
as we lift into the clouds.
Day turns to night.
The stars surround our hollow body,
shine through the buildings below.
The food on my tray is separated into plastic rectangles.
The flight attendant's smile is as canned as the air.
We watch movie after movie
to dull our minds into forgetting
that we have left the earth.
We are cheating time and the laws of gravity.
Who convinced us we were birds?
Who told us we could migrate in one day?
Our bodies travel easily.
Our minds are often left
in the space between the heavens
and the earth.

I fall asleep for a moment

Wake covered in sweat.
Mind swirling like an eddy, pulling me deeper
into darkness. Stomach unsettled.

I take a sip of water.
Cass and Agatha snore beside me.
Silk masks and fuzzy blankets.
Cuddling like newborn puppies.
I have too much on my mind to join the pile.
Cynthe is watching a movie about gangsters.
Bullets explode into the crowd at a speakeasy.
A woman in a sequin dress
throws herself in front of her lover.
I wave.
Cynthe responds with resting bitchface.

I stand and stretch my legs, see Professor Jenkins
in the back, near the lavatory.
Just seeing her calms me.
She's doing knee bends.
She dips and stretches, leg lunges down the aisle.

This trip gets harder the older you get.
I should have worn my compression socks.
She looks at me sideways. *Can't sleep?*
No, I say.
I don't want to tell her that my body won't rest.
My body feels unsafe, pummeling through time and space.
Every time I try to relax, I cannot breathe.
I want to talk about something, someone else.
Not me.

I'm thinking about Barbara.
I wish there was more written about her.
More records found.

She releases a low whistle through her lips.
That's the hard part about history.
So much is unknown. So much is lost.

I pull my neck from side to side, take another swig of water.
Everyone has a different opinion about who she was,
her relationships, her music, her experiences.
How do we know the truth?

Jenkins laughs and stretches her arms across her chest.
First the right, then the left, and says,
What is truth?

She reaches down to touch her toes.
History is always interpretation.
We try our best to be accurate,
to create logical stories with what we find.

She raises her eyebrows, and her eyes twinkle with mischief.
Did you know that there are still manuscripts out there?
Barbara wrote eight opuses, but we think one is missing.
It's mentioned in several texts, but we don't know if it exists.

I look at her with wide eyes.
That's crazy.

She continues, *I know. It's exciting.*
Scholars believe it must be lost in a stack somewhere.
Just waiting for someone to uncover it.

The thought of that makes my neck tingle.
I imagine Indiana Jones searching through
a dusty, hidden Venetian library,
accompanied by a female scholar
wearing a dashing linen vest and matching skirt.

Anyway, as for truth, Jenkins says,
we can try to understand the historical context of Venice at the time.
We can find birth documents, death documents.

We attempt to study her life—we can research clothing,
customs, politics, marital laws, but we can never fully fathom
her true motivations, or her relationships.

Even though we make an effort to understand her experiences
as a woman during this time, we will never be able to comprehend
her limitations and freedoms. These are things
we cannot fully grasp with our twenty-first-century minds.

A flight attendant squeezes by us,
takes her seat, slips off her heels,
and starts flipping through a *People* magazine.

I look over at Cynthe's screen.
The woman in the sequins is now holding the machine gun.
Sipping a bottle of gin, grinning at the scared gangsters
standing in her way.

I bite the tip of my thumb, feeling sad for a moment.
I wish I could meet her.

Jenkins crosses her arms, hugs herself.
Me too.

In the end, we modern listeners
want her to be a martyr, a cipher, a genius, a whore—
she closes her eyes—*and a saint.*

She pauses and places her hand on my arm.
I think she was only one woman, doing her best
to share her art with the world.

I lean back in my seat

Close my eyes.
Barbara's image comes into my mind.
The one painting created in her lifetime.
Her cheeks ruddy, flowers in her hair,
ample breasts exposed, nipple
barely hidden under a layer of lace,
draped in red satin.
Rings adorn her fingers.
Not quite innocent.
What could she tell me,
if she parted her lips in song?

My body jerks forward

as the wheels hit the ground.
We disembark.

Agatha's sleep mask is still on her forehead.
Cass's hair is matted in the back.
Jenkins stretches her calves and glutes.
Cynthe walks with her eyes closed.
Brick chews on a toothbrush.
Madison looks fresh, and just to prove it,
opens a compact to admire her complexion.
I drag my fingers through my hair
and pop a piece of gum.

The customs agent grins as he bludgeons
my passport with a stamp.
Benvenuto a Venezia.

We take a bus through the small towns.
Children riding their bikes wave to us.
We park at the Piazzale Roma.
Everyone scrambles to buy vaporetto tickets.

The water bus arrives.
Jenkins smiles, and whispers into my ear,
Squeeze your way up to the front!
I look at Agatha, trapped in the crowd.
I wave, and she looks at me, wide-eyed
with fear.

I push my way to the bow of the boat,
find an empty seat, awkward with my wheely suitcase.
The conductor unties the boat, kicks off the dock,
rolls the steering wheel to the left,
and navigates to the entrance
of the Grand Canal.

Everyone on the boat gasps

as we turn down
    a wide waterway filled with motoring boats
        and floating taxis.
           Gondoliers sway,
sporting black-and-white-striped T-shirts,
    ribboned straw hats. They dip their oars
        and lean
           into the waves,
as tourists beam,
    sitting on velvet cushions
        sunk down into the smooth, black hulls
           of the bobbing boats.
The waterway defies logic
    as we steer our way
        through the liquid traffic,
           travel back through centuries,
craning our necks to see the skyline,
    the arched windows.
        Stone-walled palazzi carved
           with family crests, banners, and flags.
History entering our lungs.
    A world of art
        that we see,
           and taste in the salty air.
The water and weeds
    swirl beneath our boat.
        A whisper of a past that is present.
        Music we long to hear.

We land at the Ca' d'Oro

Agatha looks green. She's gulping air
as we wheel our suitcases to Strada Nuova.
Jenkins motions to the wide lane packed
with people and shops.

This is the busiest street in Venice.

We pass restaurants teeming with tourists.
I can smell the garlic and oil as I watch them twirl
sepia-ink pasta, crack open clams, and dip bread into sauce.
We walk past a steeple with church bells ringing,
and see the sign for Hotel Giorgione.

The suited man at the desk hands us heavy keys
attached to red tassels.

Agatha and I high-five. *Roomies!*

Cass shoots us a panicked, wide-eyed look
as he realizes he and Brick are bunked together.

Cynthe narrows her eyes at Madison,
and says, *No,*
firmly shoving Brick and Madison together.
She hands them a key, then links arms with Cass.
Roomies? she asks him.
All right, but I snore, he jests,
and hefts his backpack onto his shoulder.
At least you're not a little bitch,
Cynthe replies under her breath.

Madison purses her lips and turns to the stairs.
Brick flips his thumbs up, lifts one eyebrow, and says,
Looks like Venice really is for lovers.
Cynthe holds up her middle finger
and then shoves it down her throat, gagging.

Our room is hilarious

a cheaper, gaudy version of Venice opulence,
a puke-green floral pattern stenciled on the wall,
trying but failing to replicate
the delicate cut velvet fabrics of the city.
Two-dimensional brass headboards
painted behind the twin beds
covered in thin, worn blankets,
flat, sad pillows.

But as we pry the windows open
and hear the murmur of the crowds below,
the sounds of bells and gondoliers ringing out
to each other, we whoop with excitement.

Agatha jumps onto the bed. *We're here!*

She grabs the bottle of prosecco
she purchased in the airport,
unwraps the golden foil,
and nudges the cork with her thumb.

Pop!

She pours the bubbles into plastic hotel cups.
I hold my glass high. *Benvenuto a Venezia!*
Salut! We clink glasses.

I take a fizzy sip,
and let out a deep sigh,
filled with excitement and relief.

12
Barbara

Venice, Italy
1635

I awake in my new room

Satin sheets
soft against my cheek.

Fresh nightgown
draped around my frame.

The gold brocade fabric
from the tailor's shop
hung across
the open window.

The same fabric
covers the four-poster bed.

Out of everything
in this new life,
I enjoy the mornings
the most.

Quiet.
No chores.

A moment to simmer
like a pot,
before the day begins.

I close my eyes.
Breathe deeply.
Feel gratitude.

I study
the dust particles floating
in the light,
the sounds from the canal below.

I close my eyes
and run my hands
along my body,
feel my collarbone,
my soft skin.

Mancini barges through the door

Look at you!

Lying in bed,
while others work!

Don't get used to this!

You'll be back in the kitchen
after they've had their fun
with you.

I blush and pull the covers higher,
over my breasts.

She shoves a tray
into my lap.

Cornetti and buns,
dishes filled with butter and jam,
dark purple grapes
and poached pears.

A soft-boiled egg,
resting high on a pillar.

And my favorite,
a pot of melted chocolate.

You'd better fatten up!

They don't like
their girls too skinny!

She cackles down the hall.

Each week I improve

My fingers are callused.
My voice is more agile.

I have completed a whole song.
Now Cavalli plays the counterparts.

When the two lutes play
against each other,

I sway in my chair.
My foot can't keep still.

Our voices blend
on corresponding lines.

My pulse beats,
muscles twitch,
music builds,
passion rises.

I am becoming.

Stronger.

Nicolò takes me

to see a different historical site
after each lesson.

We talk about our lives,
and our experiences.

We talk about the plague
and the outbreak
four years ago.

Only the strong survived.

Back then, Mamma and I
were sick for a month,
isolated.

Rossini fed us broth,
as we hovered
in our fever dreams,
on the brink of death.

We talk
about the floating churches
built to pray
for the banishment of evil
wickedness.

Churches that blamed
the prostitutes
and sinners
and sodomites
for the spread of the disease.

The preachers
who still scream
their truth for anyone who needs
someone to blame.

As we walk,
we talk about the bodies.

Carted out of homes
in wheelbarrows.

Bodies stacked
on the side of the road.

So many bodies,
they are buried under the stones
in each public square.

We walk among the dead.

We pray the plague
will not return.

We stop at a printer's shop

I see the men in aprons
setting type
rolling press drums
drying sheets of paper
on the line.

The ink smells strong
and musty,
like blood.

Ciao, Nicolò!

A man in an apron waves.
Nicolò waves back.

This is my home.

You live in a printing press?

He smiles and points
to the apartment above.

I live there.

*This is one of the finest printing shops
in all of Italy.*

*They have printed the works
of all the greatest musicians.*

*Gabrieli.
Caccini.
Monteverdi.*

Can I see it?

> *What? The press?*

Your apartment.

> *No!*

Why not?

> *It's not appropriate.*
> *I've never had a lady in my room before.*

Aha!
I laugh.
You forget,
I'm not a lady!

He bites his lip,
and looks
down the alley
both ways.

> *Okay. You can see it.*

He puts his finger in the air.

> *Briefly.*
> *But then you must go. . . .*

Before he can finish
his sentence,
I've grabbed his hand
and started up
the stairs.

I'm amazed at what I see

It's one room.

Filled with books
stacked on the floor.

A desk with paper and ink.
A stool and music stand.

A lute.
A trumpet.
A penny whistle.
A drum.

A nightstand with a bowl
and a pitcher of water
for washing.

A small bed.

There's not even a dining table
and chairs.

I thought you were rich!

I blurt out,
and then immediately
feel ashamed.

He flushes
and begins to pick up the papers
spread across the floor.

> *Why in the world
> would you think that?*

He replies calmly,
still not making eye contact.

*Because you're friends
with Ferrante and Loredano,
and you belong to the academy.*

He lets out a sarcastic huff.

> *Ferrante and Loredano
> are not my friends.*

What are they, then?

> *Loredano is my patron.*

> *Ferrante is his best friend,
> and the secretary of his estate.*

> *He gloms on to Loredano
> like an eel to coral.*

Loredano is your patron?

Yes.
He helps me.
Pays for me.
Introduces me.

I thought you were a lord.
A nobleman!

Oh, I am.
But only in name.

My father impregnated
his best friend's wife.

When she was shunned,
he gave me his name,
and paid for us to live in a small house
in another town.

I have no inheritance,
but I have a crest.

I walk around the room.

Touch the items
on his desk.

Slide my fingers
across the strings of the lute.

I look at him,
with sorrow.
I didn't know.

His face contorts,
fills with anger.

> *And who are you*
> *to judge me?*

he says softly,
balling up his fist.

> *You're a servant!*

> *At least*
> *I have my freedom!*

> *And a name!*

I hold my tongue.

Calm my anger.
Stare at him hard.

Yes. You have your freedom.
I never will.

My eyes fill with tears.

Even
if I weren't a servant,
even
if I had a father,
even
if I were your wife,
even
if you gave me your name.

I would not have freedom.

> *My wife?*

he whispers.

Moves his body closer,
takes one finger,
and tilts my head
so my eyes
meet his.

Is that what you want?

No.

Tears spill down my cheeks.

I don't know.

I want to make music.

*I don't want
to be anyone's property.*

*And yet,
I am everyone's property.*

His eyes
connect with mine.

Flowing sea moss,
grass, and sage.

Dark hair falls
across his light brown skin.

Hand on my cheek,
jaw clenched and strong,
full lips parted.

He is beautiful.

I'm sorry.
I had no right to yell.

I . . . I am ashamed.
For my actions . . .
and my poverty.

He separates from me.

You're smart, and you feel . . .
everything.

Joy, music, pain, anger.

I wish I could offer you something.

A life.
A prospect.

An opportunity to leave
your house,
servitude.

But as you see,
I have nothing.

I walk closer to him.

You are ashamed.
You think I am judging you.
You think you have nothing,
but you don't understand.

What don't I understand?

This room.
This place.

*Now I know
why you defended me.*

*Why you fought for me.
Why you want to help me.*

It makes me understand you more.

It makes me . . . like you more.

His face crumples,
and I see tears in his eyes.

> *I have nothing to give . . .
> to any woman.*

> *Nothing to give to you.*

I take one step
closer
until our lips
are almost touching.

Yes, you do.

I close my eyes,
and press my lips to his.

Ashamed

I gasp,
turn away from him,
and hold my lips.

Oh, God.
I kissed him.

Just as I'm about to run,
he grabs me by the waist.

Spins me to face him,
crushes his mouth
to mine.

Chest to chest.
Stomach to stomach.
I feel him press.
Hard.

I lose my breath.
Gasping.

Soften.

Open myself to him.

He wraps
around me.
I can feel the muscles
in his chest,
his back.

Strong.
Wanting.
Warm.

He pulls back

His eyes widen.

I can't talk.
I can only giggle,
and hold my lips.
Oh, Nicolò.

He lifts his eyebrows,
smiles in shock,
and starts laughing too.

> *You must go.*

> *I don't seem to be able
> to talk, or walk, or
> control myself.*

I laugh again.

*Okay, you beast.
Take me home.*

He reaches for the door.
I grab his hand.

We walk down
the winding steps.

Nicolò twirling me
against the cold stone wall,
breathing together
sneaking kisses
wanting more
together
closeness
as we descend.

(CHORUS)

Dream:

a shadow twitches

across the sky

alone on a stage

the night is a theater

stars, punched from holes

in the painted heavens above

sand shifts

the lagoon surrounds

twirling skirts

flowing water

the heat

the pressure

the lights

a performance

is an act

of love

13

Lula

Venice, Italy
2025

After a blurry evening

and a jet-lagged night of sleep,
Agatha and I arrive at the hotel breakfast room,
ready for our first day exploring Venice.

The tables are covered in white tablecloths
packed with cornetti, white rolls, and nutty breads,
petite pots of jam and Nutella,
cases filled with salami and ham, muesli, and milk.
A machine spurts and froths foamed milk for espresso.
Fresh squeezed orange juice sloshes in pitchers.

Yummmmmm! says Agatha, dashing for a plate.

Check this out! Brick exclaims
as he smashes a metal tube into the softest part of a roll
and fills it with white cream.
Reminds me of last night! he says as he eyes Madison.
Cynthe spits her cheese onto her plate.
Even Madison looks disgusted.

All right, everyone, Jenkins says, *you have some free time,
and then we will rendezvous for the opera at sixteen hundred.
I'm so excited that we get to see Monteverdi's* L'Orfeo!
*The story of Orpheus and Eurydice, written in 1607.
It was one of the first operas, and yet it has survived
for centuries. What a gift to be able to see it in Venice!*

I take a few hours to myself

much to Agatha's and Cass's chagrin.

Are you sure? They look concerned.
I need some time to think, I respond.

I shiver when I step outside.
The cool air fills my lungs.
Every follicle of my body awakens.

For the first time in a very long time,
I feel like I can breathe.

Pigeons gather at my feet, guide my way
along the hidden passageways, canal after canal.

At first I look at the map,
and then I allow myself to get lost
amid the ringing bells, the children laughing,
laundry hung overhead.

I plant my feet on the stones.
I feel like I might grow wings,
become an angel or a ghost.

The present and the past are alive
behind every corner.

Rupture and rapture.

In the eyes of the gargoyles,
the open mouths of the statues.

Something grows inside me.
Dangerous and free.
A lion, with broken chains.

Time clicks on the clock tower gears.
It has been here far longer than me,
and when I am done living,
it will remain.

The light shines on the faces of the passing people.
Marble sculptures walk above water.
All is alive with movement.

Shadows and passion.

Everything in the city covered in salt.
I can feel the crystals growing across every surface.
The bridges, the walls.

If I stand here long enough,
I will become the sea.

At the hotel

Professor Jenkins gleams
in an elegant, opalescent gray gown
that glints with pink highlights as she turns.
She looks like the main character in an opera.
I imagine her in her youth, on the stage.
Flowers thrown at her feet.

From my all-black wardrobe
I have chosen a pencil skirt and a turtleneck.
Formal and indistinct, but it fits me well
and accentuates my curves.
I've smoothed my auburn hair into a side knot,
and I let Agatha apply a thick line
of cherry red to my lips.

You look like you're going to a funeral, says Madison.
She's dressed in a strapless, flesh-colored,
see-through dress,
embroidered with pastel flowers
and green tendrils clutching the side of her breasts,
just enough to cover her nipples.

Well, you look like a pernicious weed, says Agatha.
Agatha is covered in golden glitter,
a nymph who has paused,
on its way to play its harp, in a crested wave.
Her sun-bleached wavy curls
cascading down her back.

My breath catches when Cass arrives,
dressed in a tuxedo, a black shirt, and black bow tie.
His amber eyes glinting like sunlight.

James Brickerton the Third
bounds down the stairs in a white tuxedo blazer
and a flower-print bow tie
that perfectly complements Madison's ensemble.

I can see them in twenty years, middle-aged,
unhappily married, drinking martinis at the club.

Where is Cynthe? Jenkins looks at her watch.
I always get lost on my way to the theater.
We have to leave now.
She looks at Cass, who shrugs.

Cynthe arrives seconds later in a belted kimono.
Black silk embroidered with silver birds.
A contrasting magenta obi tied tight around her waist,
accentuating her honey skin and pink hair.

Cynthe, you look stunning, I say, and I mean it.
She shrugs, and responds,
It was my grandmother's. She grew up in Kyoto.
Agatha and I smile and exchange glances,
shocked that Cynthe has shared something about herself.

All right, team! Let's get walking!
Jenkins puts on her glasses and pulls out her map.
We snake through the alleyways, eliciting stares.

A waiter, leaning against a door, shouts,
Bellisima! as I pass.
I blush. I'm not used to compliments.

Cass glares at the man.

We pause to take ridiculous photos at the Rialto Bridge.
Posing like prom kids.
Agatha takes one of me and Cass.
Sun shining on our faces.
Black clothing against the white backdrop of the famous bridge.

He hooks his arm around my waist as she snaps the photo.
You look radiant, he says, and kisses me on the cheek.
My heart flutters like the sun glinting off the lagoon.

La Fenice

The crowd gathers on the steps.
Men who look like they've just stepped away
from a *GQ* photoshoot on a yacht.
Women who look red-carpet ready
draped in silk and organza,
floating in a cloud of Chanel No. 5.
Jenkins tell us of the history
of La Fenice, the Phoenix.
How it burned down in the nineties and then was rebuilt.
A man in a tuxedo appears on the stairs,
rings a small bell to alert us
it's time to take our seats.
The cream-colored lobby is fitted
with marble columns and cut-crystal chandeliers.
Huge vases full of lilies mark the two staircases.
I glance at *il pompiere*, the firefighters in uniforms,
arms crossed, prepared for the stage
to light up the night.

Our tickets are not together

Jenkins says. *Does anyone mind being by themself?*
Holding one ticket in her hand.

I take a deep breath.
I can do it, I say.

Everyone looks at me in shock.

I'm trying to be more independent,
I say, and grab the ticket.
It will be good for me.

Jenkins raises her eyebrows,
and silently hands two tickets to Brick and Madison,
who head off to box seats around the hallway,
a pair to Cass and Agatha, who smile,
but glance at me sheepishly.

I take a breath. *I'll be fine. Don't worry.*
Agatha takes my hand. *Are you sure?*
Yes, I say, trying to convince myself.

Jenkins pats me on the back.
We'll be right next door.
Let me know if you need me.

I take one more breath, turn the door handle,
and open a box directly in front of the stage,
high above the ground.

I enter and close the door

Enveloped in darkness, my eyes blur
with gold and red velvet before me.
I walk to the edge and grasp the railing.
Lean forward inhaling each gilded detail.
Circular frescoes, angels with rainbow wings,
bouquets of blooming roses
encrusted with golden filigree.
So much shine.
I rotate my head to the right and the left,
an owl, trying to capture
the roll and the glint of the night.
The crowd gathers below,
hovering among the red velvet chairs.
The ceiling above, painted a light blue, heaven,
swimming with angels and seraphim.
Buonasera. I jump and look to my right.
There is a man, smiling at me.
I barely noticed him as I entered.
Now I have no idea how I could have missed him.

Buonasera

I respond, embarrassed by my gawking,
my intake of the surroundings, my abandonment.
He's smiling at me, his cut jawline
highlighting soft dark brown eyes.
He runs his hand through his light blond hair
that falls just below his chin.

You speak English? he asks me shyly.
I nod. He looks hesitant, which makes him appear
even softer, more handsome.
I try, but I'm not so good. He smiles again.

What he's wearing is strangely informal,
but it makes him look like a Ralph Lauren model.
A loose chambray shirt, linen pants, no socks, loafers,
like he's just come from a rugby match,
he's been in the sun all day, drinking gin and tonics.

I'm here with my sister. He waves to a box
across the theater, and a statuesque woman
with short black hair waves back and blows kisses.

I'm here with a group. I wave to Cass and Agatha,
and they wave back, Agatha looking at me with intensity.
I can hear her telepathically asking,
Who is that gorgeous man?!
I stare at her wide-eyed and wish I could point at him
and say, *I know! Right?!*

A group from where? he asks.
I smile and respond. *We study together
at the New England Conservatory of Music.*
He chuckles.
I'm sitting next to a musician? At the opera?
I laugh with him.
I'm a vocalist who studies baroque music.

He claps his hands together and exclaims, *Perfetto!*

I smooth my hair and ask, *Are you from Venice?*
He smiles. *Yes.*
My family has been here since the sixteen hundreds.

I have an Italian name. I point to myself. *Luciana.*
But I have no idea where our family comes from.
His eyes intensify as he rolls my name through his lips.
Luciana.

I blush. *But my friends call me Lula.*
We sit in silence for a moment.
My name is Lodovico Foscari Widmann Rezzonico.
But please, call me Vico.
I jut out my hand. *Nice to meet you, Vico.*
He laughs and takes it.
Nice to meet you, Luciana.

Feeling awkward again, I ask,
Do you like opera?
He nods enthusiastically. *I love it. Very much.*
Especially the classics. I am an artist. A visual artist.
I love to listen to music, especially opera, while I work.
My heart warms. He's an artist.

What kind of art do you create?
He wrings his hands while he tries to find the words.
Right now I'm learning to . . . He hesitates.
I don't know the word. Restaurare . . . the frescoes.
I bring history to life.

I think for a moment. *Restore? You restore frescoes?*
He nods enthusiastically. *Sì. Sì. Yes. Restore.*
I am enrolled in an apprenticeship and I'm studying.
This is good for me. Good for Venice.

There is a hush

We can hear the soft tuning of instruments.
The conductor waves to the crowd
from the orchestra pit. The light fades.
The red curtain parts, heels click onstage.
First note. The voices fill my chest and shatter
something fragile inside me.
The edges of my body fade.
I am filled with sound and light and shadow.
Tears fall down my cheeks.
I do not smooth the sweet water from my skin.
Let it linger, let it dry.
I cannot take my gaze from the dancing,
the lifting, the skirts shifting and swaying.
The breath that swells in their lungs.
Mouths open. Pain and passion.
Voices fill the hall, float in the air, surround me.
I close my eyes tight and pray for the souls
who have not heard this glorious sound.

13
Barbara

Venice, Italy
1635

I am ready

My mother dresses me
in red silk
from head to toe.

Venetian lace
around my sleeves and collar.

Slips my feet
into platform shoes.

Ties red ribbons
around my ankles, thighs.

Straps me
into a corset
that lifts and accentuates
the smooth tops
of my breasts.

Wraps and braids my hair.

Embeds strands of pearls
and rubies in a crown
around the tresses.

Long curls flowing
down one shoulder.

Powders my skin
as white as the inside
of an oyster shell.

Paints my lips
as red as a pomegranate.

We step into a gondola

filled with flowers
and fur blankets.

The driver bites his finger
and whines
like an alley cat
when he sees me.

Unable to take his eyes away
from my blooming
breasts.

He digs his oar
deep into the emerald water.
The sea grass sways.

I've dreamed of this moment
for years.

The brocade gown,
the jewels,
the attention,
the music, the sea.

When I look
at my mother's expression,
all the excitement leaves.

She's trembling.

My performance
will decide
both of our fates.

Save us,
or condemn us.

I cannot let her down.

14

Lula

Venice, Italy
2025

My eyes are closed

but I feel his hand on mine.
This man, who I barely know, has reached for me.

I look at his dark brown eyes,
and I realize that I am not the only one who is crying.

He is moved by the power of the voices,
the bodies, moving, filling hearts and chests with sound.

The palpable emotion in the air,
as the Spirit of Music welcomes the audience,
soothes us, tells us that she can *Calm every troubled heart.*
Magic, music, voices fill the room.

The nymphs and shepherds form the Greek chorus,
swirling around Orpheus as he falls in love with Eurydice.

I watch the joyful dance of marriage, the ceremony
in the temple, stealing glances at the deep brown eyes
next to me, filled with emotion, as Orpheus sings,
After grief one is more content. After pain one is happier.

Until the messenger arrives and tells Orpheus
that his new bride has been gathering flowers
in the meadow and has received a fatal snakebite.
Thou art dead, my life, and I am breathing?

I want to look at him, this stranger.
Watch him, as he watches the stage.

Orpheus places a spell on the boat man,
and charms Persephone with his singing.
Hades tells him to take his love,
return to the world of the living,
but *a single glance will condemn him to eternal loss.*

I tell myself, Don't look back.
Don't look back. Look at the stage.
Look at the hope and heartbreak before you.
I am spellbound as Orpheus, alone and unsure, asks,
How can I be sure she is following?

Don't look back.
I cannot look away.
I search for Vico's brown eyes,
and they find mine.
He squeezes my hand, as the tears flow.

Eurydice disappears into the ether,
and Orpheus rises to the surface.
Alone.

Something has changed. Here in the final chorus.
Here in the grief. A damaged body. A loss.
A rise from the underworld.

After the last note

the theater hums.
The audience waits a moment,
and erupts with applause.
I stand up. Dizzy.
Reeling with the music still inside me.

I feel like I don't know which way is up, or down,
traveling between heaven and earth.
Place my hand on a railing and feel a carving in the wood.
I peer down and see the symbols.

ᚠᛖ:ᛁ:ᛏᛁ:ᚦ

I run my thumb across the indent.
The letters are beguiling and strange.

Luciana. My eyes meet his as he says,
When will I see you again?

I try to hide my amazement. *I don't know.*
I hesitate. *I'm not sure I will have time.*
He takes my hand in his and kisses the inside of my palm.
Heat spreads across my cheeks.
I want to show you so many things.
My city. My work. He kisses my hand again.

I jump as the door slams open
and Agatha and Cass spill in.

Cass eyes Vico's lips, touching my palm.
His eyes turn even more golden.
What are you doing? Cass says in an accusing tone.
Agatha whacks her hand across his chest.
Someone call the fire brigade, she whispers to me.
It's getting HOT in here.

I introduce them to Vico.
Agatha enthusiastically shakes his hand,
and then places her other hand around his muscled biceps.

Cass turns his head and looks toward the door.
He won't look at me.
I'm about to say something when Jenkins walks in,
and gestures us out, like a mother hen.

I give Vico one last look,
and he pushes a piece of paper into my palm.
We hop down the steps.
Take our first fresh breaths of salty, outside air.

I smile when I see Vico's name
and phone number in flowing script.
I put the paper to my lips and imagine
it is his hand.

14
Barbara

Venice, Italy
1635

We arrive at Palazzo Ruzzini

A footman waits
at the canal entrance
and escorts us
into a cavernous foyer
with arched doorways.

We climb the stairs
and arrive at a grand hall.

Frescoes cover every wall.

Scenes of Grecian hillsides
painted in muted greens and browns,
the Parthenon
in the background.

In the foreground,
Aphrodite sits on a pedestal,
robe slipping off her shoulder.

There are chairs,
covered in golden velvet,
set up for the occasion.

All pointing to a single stage.

My stage.

Well, look what the tide washed in

I turn
and see Loredano.

He's exiting a large room
covered in bookcases.

In the center
of his study
is a globe of the world
the size
of two grown men.

Ferrante is right behind him.
He pats signore on the back.

My lord, Strozzi!

*How well
you have transformed
our little kitchen wench
into a buxom prostitute!*

I'm not—a—
I stammer,
while my mother calms me
with her hand.

Signor Strozzi
laughs and inhales
a pinch
from his snuffbox.

My dear Ferrante.

*How mistaken you are!
You cheapen her.*

As we know,
she has been tutored
and trained by the best.

I promise you, she will exceed
your expectations.

Ferrante pulls out a handkerchief
and wipes his mustache.

The only expectation
I have for her
is in the boudoir!

I feel like
I might empty
the contents of my stomach
onto the floor.

I imagine her preferences
to be as base
as her station in life.

Not at all like my own.

Ah, yes,
Ferrante,
your preferences precede you.

And terrify schoolboys
across the land.

Strozzi motions
to the entrance.

Oh look, our audience arrives!

Men begin to fill the hall
and take their seats.

I scan the room
for Nicolò.

Where is he?

I cannot see him
among the crowd.

    Barbara!

Signor Strozzi
grabs my arm.

    You must meet Atto Macini,
    a castrato from Rome.

    We have extended an invitation
    to sing at the Teatro Novissimo
    when it opens.

    Atto is a performer of the highest caliber.
    Absolutely one of a kind!

My eyes connect
with a young person.

Dressed in a waistcoat
and tights like a nobleman.

Delicate features
accentuated
with powder, lip rouge,
and dark kohl lines drawn
around the eyes.

Large freshwater pearls
dangle
from earlobes.

A spray of seed pearls
decorates the lapel.

Atto's spine is straight.

The power and poise
of a Roman emperor.

The grace, beauty,
and style
of an empress.

My breath catches.

> *It's an honor to meet you,*
> *Signorina Valle.*
> *I'm excited to see this performance.*

Unsure what to say
to this dazzling creature,
I try my best.

Thank you.
I'm honored you are here.

Atto pulls me in closer,
whispers into my ear.

> *I hear there's a bet going.*
>
> *I for one know what it's like*
> *to be at the whim*
> *of these elite baboons,*
> *especially Ferrante.*

*And I want you to know
that I'm betting on you,
my queen.*

Atto kisses me
softly
on both cheeks,
and leaves me
with a sly wink.

I want to follow.

I know we're going to be
friends.

Butterfly wings flutter

in my head.

I walk to the windows.

Exit onto the balcony,
and gaze at the square below.

As the church bells ring
in the tower,
I see Nicolò running.

Just as I am
about to shout his name,
he looks up,
and stops running.

He stares at me
for a long moment
with his hand on his chest.

I lift my hand
and place it on my heart
as well.

He flashes
a broad smile,
and starts running again
toward me.

15

Lula

Venice, Italy
2025

The vaporetto is packed

My anxiety creeps in.
I think about Patience and imagine her office.
The thought of her voice makes me feel calmer.
I remember the exercises she has taught me.
I tap my forehead, my chest. Breathe.

I'm jostled and pushed against unknown men and women.
Strange smells. Armpits and cologne.
Sweat drips down my cleavage.
Separated from the others,
I feel like a shell rolling on the ocean floor.

I see Agatha pressing her nose to a cracked window,
trying to breathe fresh air. Her skin has taken on a green hue.
I wave, hoping to make her feel better.
She shoots me a look of sheer horror.

At the Ponte dell'Accademia stop, Jenkins waves her hands,
and we push our way to the front of the boat,
past older women fanning themselves, strollers, and toddlers,
and a dog tied to a traveler's backpack with a rope.

On dry land, we climb the steps of the bridge
that spans across the entire Grand Canal.
Agatha, still green, turns to Jenkins.
Why couldn't we have chosen a festival in Vienna?
Jenkins holds out her hands.
Because Vienna doesn't have this.

We reach the center of the wooden bridge.
Colorful, ancient buildings line the banks of the canal.
The dome of Basilica di Santa Maria della Salute stands regally, marking where the canal ends, and the ocean begins.

We enter the Gallerie dell'Accademia

Everything is art in this museum.
From the inlaid marble floor
to the ceiling decorated with hundreds of diamond tiles.
We enter a room filled with religious triptychs,
paintings separated into three panels.
Each of the panels is gilded in gold.

Agatha turns green again.
Oh my God.
She points to a painting of a woman
holding a golden chalice, riding a many-headed dragon,
projectile-vomiting blood from her mouth.

What's in that golden cup? asks Brick.
Looks like she's had a rough night.
He elbows Cass in the ribs and whispers,
Is she doing the medieval walk of shame?
Cass rolls his eyes. *Dude.*

Cynthe takes one for the team.
Rough night.
That's one way to describe the apocalypse.
She points to a depiction of skeletons
ensconced in flames, holding Bibles.
These were the assholes at the party who messed with her.

Jenkins, overhearing the discussion,
chuckles and chimes in.
You know, Cynthe isn't wrong.
Many of the artists of the Renaissance and baroque periods
layered their art with symbolism and nuance.

She gestures to the three panels.
A painting that seems religious
could be a representation of the political climate at the time.

The artist places the popular politicians in heaven with God.
She points to a depiction of God in heaven,
surrounded by the prophets and his devoted followers.
And the unpopular politicians and households
in hell . . . with Satan.

Wicked, says Brick.
Literally, says Cynthe.

My brain is overflowing

with new knowledge and beauty and art.

We visit the Ospedale della Pietà.
One of the most famous musical sites in all of Venice,
where Antonio Vivaldi led
his famous group of students,
the *figlie del coro,* the chorus daughters.

I walk to the side of the building to see the *scafetta,*
a little window where infants were left.

I read from the brochure.
Daughters of prostitutes, plague orphans.
The girls were taught to play musical instruments and sing.

For many it must have felt like a prison.
I shiver.

We walk to Piazza San Marco.

Visit the golden glittering cathedral,
the doge's palaces and dungeons, the Bridge of Sighs.
I am overwhelmed with the beauty and the cruelty.

Finally we enter the Biblioteca Marciana
and the Museo Correr. I scan the frescoes, the reliefs,
the human-sized globes covered in maps
of the earth and the heavens.

Unable to walk anymore, I sit on a bench
in front of a glass case.

Something catches my eye

PE:I:TI:A

I traced my thumbs over these letters
at La Fenice.
Carved into wood.
I stand and look at the display,
read the captions underneath the glass.

We believe Reitia was worshipped by a female cult
that built a sanctuary for her and brought votive offerings.

Reitia was a merciful and benevolent mother goddess.
A triple goddess. Representing all the stages of a woman's life.

I look down at my ring.
Trace it with my fingers.

Reitia is often seen in sculptures and carvings holding a key.
She is the great decider of who will be allowed to cross
between earth and the afterlife, and who will walk between.

I'm so lost in the description, I jump
when Cass slides up beside me.

What did you find? he asks, and smiles.
I'm not quite sure, I say. *It's a description
of an ancient Veneto goddess and her female cult.*
Nice! he says, and reads alongside me.

We often see Reitia represented with infinity symbols,
trees, and water, the mythology of death and resurrection.

Agatha crosses the room and joins us.
She leans on my shoulder and peers into the case.
Ooooh! Ancient goddess shit. Yes!

She reads out loud,
*It is believed that women and girls were taught in these sanctuaries
to become priestesses of Reitia. They came in large numbers
from all over the world, performed rites and ceremonies,
and taught writing and magic to women. Pilgrims celebrated together.
They danced, played music, sang, and feasted.*

I look at the display filled with bronze votives
covered in green patina. I imagine the women
that worked to cut and carve these objects.
Traveled to these sacred spots.

In the glass case there's an intricate sculpture of a devotee
with her arms open in a gesture of prayer,
a flared skirt with embroidered hem,
a diamond-shaped belt, and high boots.

Agatha continues,
Most important, Reitia is seen as a healer.
Worshippers would bring votives
of the body part that they needed healed,
such as legs, arms, and feet.

Without thinking, I touch my throat.
As I pull my hands away, I notice Agatha watching me.
She looks back at the case and reads,

The sanctuaries built in her honor
invoked the protection of the goddess,
offered miracles and hope.

Goddess of the earth and body. Goddess of writing.
Goddess of music. Goddess of healing.

Agatha, always in tune, touches my hand.
I think we should start building a healing shrine right away.
I chuckle and respond, *I'm taking notes.*

A woman joins us at the display case

She's wearing a uniform and a museum name tag.
I can see you're interested in Reitia, she says.
She seems too young to be working in a museum.
She has dreadlocks that are wound around her head
and earrings made from large chunks of amber.
Her necklace is a silver spiral.
*Some people believe that there is still an active community
that gathers and prays to the goddess.*
She winks and continues,
But it's often difficult to know what is truth and what is rumor.

As we're about to leave

she points to my hand.
That's a lovely ring you are wearing.
Do you know where it comes from?

I twist the carved red stone on my finger.
It was my mother's ring.
She told me it's been in my family for many years.

The woman nods with approval and says,
Objects like that, passed from one generation to another,
hold a lot of power and history.
They are often keys to our past.

I twist the ring again.

She laughs. *Now you can see why I work in a museum.*
I love ancient objects.
She motions to the other cases.

I study history at Università Ca' Foscari.
My focus is the Bronze Age.
The period these votives come from.
Is that the university in Venice? I ask.
Yes, she says.
We're music students from Boston, I respond.

Agatha tugs on my arm. *I think the others are moving.*
I say thank you and wave to the woman as we're leaving.
She waves, and then presses her palms
together in prayer, brings them to her forehead,
to her heart, and then bows.

A lightning bolt runs
from the bottom of my spine to the top of my head.

A connection between us.
I don't know how to name.

The vaporetto sways

I lean against the cool window.
Tired from a long day.
The buildings along the canal blur in my vision.
I close my eyes.
Half asleep, half awake.
My mother weaves in and out of my dreams.
Reading me a book at bedtime.
Smiling in the audience.
Alone beside my hospital bed.
Why am I here?
Why did Jenkins let me come?
I have nothing to contribute.
I think about the devoted priestesses.
Embroidered dresses and diamond-shaped belts.
Gathered in the mountains. Gathered near water.
Drinking, dancing, composing, singing,
offering their art. Asking for help.
For another chance. Another life.
I wish I knew how to pray.
To ask. To sing.
I am the one who needs healing.
I am the one who needs rebirth.

15

Barbara

Venice, Italy
1635

Welcome, gentlemen!

To my hearth and home.

Loredano stands
at the front of the hall,
his back to me.

He addresses the audience
with open arms.

*As always,
we gather as an academy,
with an eagle eye
on intellectual discourse,
and the pursuit
of logic, truth, and beauty!*

*We, the Accademia degli Incogniti,
dedicate all our inquiry
to the Unknown God
always in our midst.*

Today we ask the question:

*Can a common kitchen maid,
with some training,
sing to us and move us
to the point of tears?*

*Or is she
just a pigeon masquerading
as a peacock?*

*A maid
dressed as a whore?*

The men in the audience chuckle.

I want to sink into a hole.

*Listen to her,
and hold these questions
in your mind and heart.*

Without further ado . . .

Barbara Valle.

I must make them weep

For my lack of fortune
my impossible love
my desire
my innocence
my isolation.

I must make them weep

For every woman.

Who has no choice
who is used
who is abandoned
who has been forgotten.

I must make them weep

For their lack of love.

Their selfishness
their greed
their lust for power
their privilege.

I must make them see

Beyond their gold
violence,
beyond body and time.

I must make them weep.

My whole body trembles

as I take my seat,
the borrowed lute
on my lap.

Trying not to cry.

I look for Nicolò.
His eyes steady me,
as liquid and green
as the lagoon.

Atto, my new friend,
holds my gaze.

I feel the camaraderie.
The encouragement.

One musician to another.

> *I see Cavalli*
> *has not helped her*
> *with her nerves,*

Ferrante grumbles for all to hear.

Strozzi tries to defend me.

> *Give her a moment, Ferrante.*
> *It's her first time.*

> *Yes, we all know*
> *how skittish and shy*
> *a girl becomes*
> *when it's her first time.*

More laughter in the crowd.

I search for my mother.

Her expression is hard,
anchored.

Her eyes do not leave me.
I know she is with me.

I wrote this song.
It is mine to sing.

My spine
becomes a steal rod
shooting toward the sky.

Just like Cavalli taught me

I run my fingertips
hard on the gut strings,
once.

A stark introduction.

And release a guttural sound
slowly from my throat.

Hold the vowel
and work my way down the scale,
voice mimicking weeping.

A pierced angel falling,
mourning the loss
of heaven.

    Lagrime mie.

My tears.

I fill my lungs with air
and let the sacred
serum
seep out
one push at a time.

My body moves
against the lute
with each rush of sound.

Pulse, then hush.
Pulse, then hush.

Lagrime mie, à che vi trattenete?

My tears, why do you hold back?

I use all the power in my lungs
and enunciate with fierce precision.

I lighten and soften,
lift slowly,
light, so light,
longing
to approach
the heavens again
with my feathered wings
so tender.

My tears are rising.

I fill my lungs again,
feral, untamed,

spitting
a slow recitative chant.

> *Sta la bella innocente,*
> *dove giunger non può raggio di sole.*

The beautiful innocent one is enclosed,
where sunrays can't reach her.

I slide down the scale,
a lost feather floating,
wafting on the gusts
of air.

Again,
my voice, my lament
rips through the air,
pleading.

E voi, lumi dolenti, non piangete?

And grieving eyes, you don't weep?

I ride the edge of the wind.

My voice so soft,
it may break.

Each word
a ragged crack.

The hair lifts
on the back of my neck.
I feel the energy pulse
in the room.

My voice catches.
I cannot weep.

Not here.
Not in front of them.

I hold everything
close, contained
until the last moment,
and then I release
it all.

All the fear, the love,
the rage.

Lagrime mie, à che vi trattenete?

My tears, why do you hold back?

I trill and swoop.

My voice
falls from the sky.

Finished.

I cannot hold back my tears.

My energy gone.
My wings torn.

And I,
the fallen angel,
land
on the earth.

Before the applause begins

I know
that I have broken
through the veil.

I know I have left earth
for a moment,
and I have connected
with something holy.

I don't need to look up
to see the tears.

I am a mouthpiece.
A cipher.
An oracle.

I am worthy.
I was born to create.

Worshipping
at the altar
of beauty.

I will spend my life
singing
and weeping.

Grateful.

I am here.

I leave the stage

Ferrante finds me,
grips my arm.

Hard.

I know there will be
a bruise.

He turns me around.
Pushes me toward the open window
onto the balcony.

Leans me over the railing.

Thrusts
into my backside,
places his palm
on the back of my neck.

My stomach turns
at the potential plummet.
The square below.

You lost, I say
with all the courage
I can muster.

He presses against my skirts
and holds me there.

The air leaves my stomach.

> *I will pay your master,*

he hisses.

*And then
we can find a way
for you to pay off
the hundred ducats
you've cost me.*

He releases me.
His thumbprints remain
on my neck.

I take a moment

Before I greet my mother,
my audience.

Before I see
Nicolò's elation.

Before he kisses my hand.

Before Strozzi lifts me
from the floor
and shouts with joy.

Before Atto
kisses me on the cheek
and invites me
to visit
Palazzo delle Delizie.

I take a moment
to look at the lights.

To remember the feeling,
the connection.

To remember
how I felt just moments ago.

Before Ferrante
threatened me.

Before I felt
dirty
worthless
ashamed.

I take a moment.

To wonder
how I will make him pay
for what he has done.

For what he will do.

ACT 3

16
Lula

Venice, Italy
2025

The next morning

we weave through the streets
of Cannaregio.

Take one left and a right
on a small lane labeled Calle de Remer,
and we end up in a quiet courtyard.

The ensemble looks confused and bored.
Jenkins is bursting with excitement.

She stops in front of a humble house,
with red gardenias growing in the window boxes.
This is it, she says to me, breathless, her cheeks flushed.
This is what? I ask.
She places her hand on my shoulder.
This is Barbara Strozzi's house.

I see a small gray building.
Two stories high, windows looking into the courtyard,
two entrances to the canal.

Jenkins runs her hands along the stone, closes her eyes.
Historians believe she lived in several houses in Venice.
The first palazzo was a grander estate, where we think
she and her mother, Isabella, were servants
in the house of Giulio Strozzi.

She grabs my hand and squeezes it.
But this is the house where she wrote much of her music, raised her four children, and lived with her mother.

I like to think this was the house where she may have been the happiest.

The others walk to a fruit stand

around the corner. I take my time in the courtyard.
Run my hand along the stone walls. I imagine her here.
Windows open, her voice drifting through the air, like steam
rising off the canal in the morning. I feel comfort and love
pulsing through the metal, the stone. The wrought-iron grates
on the oval-shaped windows, the salt and rust
that have chipped away the paint, fissures, and cracks.
I can hear the music, children laughing, the gondola tied
and sloshing against the side of the dock, as the boats pass.
I close my eyes and imagine her walking through the door.
I feel through the layers of dirt and time.

Festival registration

The Basilica dei Santi Giovanni e Paolo
is a swirl of activity.

Tables are set up with swag,
volunteers hover with clipboards,
nervous musicians lug heavy instruments.
A pipe organ moans in the background.
Colorful banners fly overhead.

Festival Internazionale di Musica Barocca.

Representatives register the groups,
hand out badges, bags filled
with T-shirts and water bottles.

One of the volunteers focuses on me.
Ciao, bella ragazza Americana.
He looks me up and down.

Cass glares and grabs my elbow.
It's okay, Cass. He's just being friendly.
I smile. The boy raises his eyebrows.

Okay, Romeo, Cass says under his breath
as he tugs me toward our group.
Agatha links arms with me too.

After we're all signed in, Jenkins addresses us.
Take a quiet moment to absorb the beauty.

I separate from the group,
transfixed by the huge marble columns,
the tombs and funeral monuments
of doges, generals, artists, and poets.

I stop under the central rose window.

I hear a woman singing alone in a side chapel

She nods at me as I enter,
but closes her eyes and keeps singing
something sacred and ancient.
Her voice fills the space,
and my eardrums pulse with the power of voice.
I remember what that feels like.
To be filled by something unnameable.
That flows through your body and lungs.
My entire body feels like it is sound.
Tears spill down my cheeks.
My fingernails dig into my palm.
I need connection. I am not whole.
I need to find my way back to myself.
I wipe my tears away.
Grazie, I whisper, and I mean it.

16
Barbara

**Venice, Italy
1635**

A note arrives

from Atto.

I have been invited
to visit Palazzo delle Delizie.

I grab my cloak
and run through the alleys,
cross bridges,
and arrive at the palazzo
filled with anticipation.

I lift the heavy
lion-headed knocker.

A bare-chested man
greets me.

His muscles,
greased with oil,
shine in the sunlight.

My eyeballs bulge.

He shows me to a room,
showered in gold and white.

Atto is splayed
on a velvet divan,
a languid cat.

While a man
in a Greek tunic,
chest painted with gold flecks,
tickles
an ostrich-feather fan
over Atto's exposed skin.

*Welcome to my slice of heaven,
my dear Barbara.*

Atto smiles slyly
and motions for
my glass
to be filled with prosecco.

After several glasses

and a lot of laughter
and celebration
about my success
as a singer,

I'm sitting on a Persian rug
with my head resting
next to Atto's,

watching
the rhythm of the fan,
feeling
dreamy.

Atto becomes serious.

>   *You know this is just the beginning.*

Of what?

>   *Your career.*

*My career of being teased
and taunted
by rich noblemen.*

I pause,
and look Atto in the eye.

*I honestly have no idea
what happens now.*

>   *You pleased them.*

*I have fulfilled my reason
for living!*

*You tease,
but you know
that is
exactly what we were born
to do.*

*I was born to please them,
because I was born a woman.*

*They cut you
and made you . . .*

*Extraordinary?
Otherworldly?
Utterly original?*

Atto cackles
and spins
a ringlet of hair
around
an index finger.

*I was not born
with this body,
but I was destined
for the stage.*

*I have vowed
to please them,
and please myself . . .*

simultaneously.

*I want everyone to be
happy cockerels.*

Atto turns deeply serious.

> *And peacocks.*

I snort.
What's that supposed to mean?

> *I don't want you to feel left out
> because of your . . .*

Atto gestures
to my skirts.

*Well, according to Loredano,
I am a pigeon,
not a peacock.*

> *You are a true artist, Barbara.*

> *Anyone can see that.*

> *And there will be many other events.*

> *Filled with rich benefactors
> and patrons.*

> *Right, Bruno?*

The man in the tunic
smiles,
leans down,
kisses Atto
on the lips.

With an open mouth.

For a while.

I cough.

*And what will I have to do
for those patrons?*

*You must learn to navigate
this world,
as a musician.*

*Find power,
where there is power.*

*I must do what my mother
and Signor Strozzi
tell me to do.*

We'll see.

Atto snaps forward.

*We should sing a duet.
Or a trio! With Nicolò!*

Yes! How lovely!

Atto pauses
and bats long eyelashes.

*I promise
Nicolò and I will help you
find your inner peacock.*

Or your cockerel.

Atto holds my gaze.

All cocks are welcome here.

We lift off the ground.

Iridescent feathers
of laughter.

Bees hum in my brain

as I walk home.

Study the surfaces
and what lies beneath.

Salt water
eats away
board and brick.

Tree roots
crack
the foundations of houses.

Insects
make their hive
in a fissure,
a break
in the wall.

An alley cat
feeds her kittens
in a nest of discarded rags.

Nature
reclaims
erodes
breaks down
reuses
for survival.

Carves a space.
Creates a den.

Within this city.
Its rules, its structure.

I must live here too.

Searching for a corner,
a place, a home.

Courtesan.
Servant.
Prisoner.

Musician.
Composer.

The strong survive.

Instinct.
Teeth.
Claws.
Cunning.

I will too.

I will break down
these structures.

Learn, and build.

A home
of my own.

Filled with my music.

I will be my own master.

When I return

still dizzy
from the prosecco
and the passionate
display
of feathers
and skin
and mouths
at Atto's apartment,

I find Nicolò standing
in the entryway.

His blue velvet tunic
makes his green eyes
swirl
like the clear waters
of the canal.

I want to swim
in them.

He lifts me up,
twirls me,
whispers into my ear.

> *I'm still replaying*
> *the moments*
> *of last night's performance*
> *over and over*
> *in my mind!*
>
> *You were brilliant!*
> *Absolutely brilliant!*

I blush.

What are you doing here?

I'm waiting for Loredano.

*He's meeting with Strozzi
to talk about the new Teatro Novissimo.*

*They want to have a plan
when Grimani brags
about Teatro San Cassiano.*

*It's going to be the first
public opera house,
ahead of the Novissimo,
and Loredano is furious.*

I stare at his lips.

I want them
to make me feel.

Something.
Anything.

What's wrong with you?

Nicolò looks concerned.

Are you okay?

I can't stop myself.

Without a word,
I grab his hand,
run down the hallway,
pull him
to my room.

Shut the door.

Simultaneously

we reach for each other
on fire
his hands
on my face
my neck
smooth
breast
flames
that lick and bite
at tender flesh
the velvet
of his lips
his vest
the brocade
pull
my dress
the silk
against the wall
soft
and hard
disappear
into
the swirl of body
his body
my breath
the ether
smoke and ruin
ash
and then
rain.

17

Lula

**Venice, Italy
2025**

Are you sure you're going to be all right?

Agatha looks worried as I pack my purse
with sunglasses, my wallet, hand sanitizer.
I'm fine, I say, and give her an exasperated glance.
She doesn't let up.
*A couple of weeks ago you could barely leave our room,
and now you want to walk around Venice alone . . .
AGAIN.*

I close my eyes and focus.
There's no way I can express to Agatha
how good I feel here.
It's not logical.
You have to trust me.
Agatha throws her hands up.
Just send me a text so I know you're okay.

She kisses me on both cheeks, and I give her a tight hug.
As I leave our room, Cass opens his door.
Where are you going?

I push by him. *Out.*

They're just trying to help,
but I need some time alone,
to feel normal.

I can't do that with Agatha and Cass
treating me like Murano glass.

17
Barbara

Venice, Italy
1635

After the concert

Mamma and signore and I
dine together every night.

White linen
silver candlesticks
and fresh-cut flowers.

We're growing plump
on chocolate truffles
and cream.

Signore tells stories
about the men in the academy
that make us blush
and laugh.

He shares wild dreams
of writing operas,
traveling to Paris,
hunting boar,
swimming
in turquoise waters,
visiting art museums
and palaces
across the world.

He wants to own
a summerhouse
on the island of Murano.

He will buy us
parasols,
bathing robes,
silk slippers.

Ball gowns.

Perfume
that smells like spring hyacinths.

Full-length silver mirrors
for our rooms.

Anything
to make us happy.

Anything
to keep me singing.

He even gives Mamma
a yellow bird.

It sings
through the bars
of its cage.

18

Lula

Venice, Italy
2025

I have made a list

of all the places I need to visit
for my research project.

I walk the streets of Cannaregio.
Barbara's neighborhood.

Sit in the church where she was baptized.

Walk past her first house, Palazzo Pesaro.
I try to imagine what she would have seen
when she looked out the arched windows.

I step into the lobby of Ca' Sagredo,
a once formidable palace, now a hotel.
A man in the lobby looks up from his desk.
Can I help you, signorina? Would you like a room?

I blush, feeling nervous.
I'm studying a musician who would have played here.

Ah! Then perhaps you would like to see the music hall?

He leads me across the red and white diamond tiles
to the two glass chandeliers that mark the staircase.

Ca' Sagredo used to be the home of one of the most
powerful families in Venice.

I look up and I'm speechless. The walls are covered
with magnificent frescoes of clouds and boulders.
Fifty-foot bodies engaged in a battle for the heavens.

These are the giants of Olympus, he says proudly.
We walk through the portico, painted in pastoral scenes,
into the music room.

I gasp.

Admiring the hundred-foot ceilings.
Statues of gods, painted, each in a frame as if in a sculpture garden.
Satyrs and angels adoring them.

*Ca' Sagredo has been an important place for the music and arts
since the sixteen hundreds.* The concierge continues,
*Sagredo was a powerful man. They say Galileo visited,
and they had many conversations.*

I look around and imagine music being played.
*The musician I'm studying dedicated an opus
to Nicolò Sagredo. Is that the same man?* I ask.

His face lights up. *Sì! Yes! That's the same man.
He became doge of Venice. The main leader of the Council of Ten.
Perhaps he was her benefactor?*

I think of Barbara, and my spine begins to tingle.
Did she sing in this room? For him? For others?
On the way out, I stop to admire a large bouquet of flowers.

I reach for a red rose to smell its aroma.
I wince.

Pricked by a thorn.
A bead of blood rises to the surface.

18

Barbara

Venice, Italy
1635

The evening air

chills my skin.

The sun has abandoned
the alleyway
in front
of Nicolò's apartment.

My hand on the door.

Listening
to the clanking
of the printing press.

The metal
sliding against metal.

Roll of the inked tympan
paper
pressing into
set type.

I hesitate.

He's not expecting me.

My thighs ache.
My heart beating.

I want to be with him.

I take a deep breath

Press on the door.

Lift my feet to meet each step.

At the entrance to his apartment,
I hesitate again.

If I enter,
there's no turning back.

I won't be able to stop
with just a kiss.

Breath pulses.
Feet shuffle.

I turn my body toward the steps.
Turn my body toward the door.

Circling.
I can't decide.

Right as I'm about to leave,
the door opens.

Nicolò is standing there.

Without a word

he sweeps me into his room,
closes the door behind him.

I breathe in citrus
and cinnamon
old pages of a book
night air
and sleep
sweat
dreaming.

19
Lula

Venice, Italy
2025

I look at the map

and locate the Santa Maria dei Derelitti,
the church of the Ospedaletto.

An ancient hospital,
home to a choir of orphaned children
during the Renaissance.

Can I enter the church? I ask a woman
poised at a desk in the entryway.

She shakes her head.
It is closed to the public because of La Biennale.

You can pay to see the contemporary art installation.

She hands me a pamphlet.

>   EUPHONIC EXPRESSIONS
>   with the music of Meredith Monk: "Walking Song"

I give her ten euros.

I am drawn into the hallway with a recording of a woman moaning.

Breathing, panting, a song without words.

Submerged in darkness

I run my hand along the black velvet curtains
hung throughout the museum.

A labyrinth of dark hallways
leading me toward the exhibition.

My heart beats faster.
I'm twisted in the cloth.

The music gets louder,
as light flickers and flashes at the end of the corridor.

A woman chanting disharmonic notes.

The velvet curtains feel like bedsheets
wrapped around my body at midnight.

It's dark.
I'm afraid I'm lost.

The velvet is soft on my cheek, on my bare arms.
I stop to rub my palms along the cloth.

Finally I enter a large, open room.
My body is free from the maze.

A video installation is projected onto all four walls
in black and white.

Naked bodies lying on the floor.
Sliding against each other like snakes.

I feel like I'm living inside the film,
limbs moving against my skin.

Light bodies.

I am a part of the movie.

The music, the chanting, the chaos.

I close my eyes, and the light and sound
dance on the insides of my eyelids.

I press my back against the wall, with my feet apart,
and my palms against the cold plaster.

Feel the beat in my breast, my thighs.

I think of Cass.

Imagine him.

Wanting.

My skin, my chest.

My head thrown back.

He turns me around, until my cheek is pressed
against the wall.

The brightness flickers around me.

Pins my hands with his hands.

Leans into me.

The images of people
moving against one another.

Kissing the back of my neck.
His hands in my hair.

His warm breath
sends a bolt of electricity through my core.

Alight with glowing movement.

The rhythm.
Breathing together.

I fall into the shadow,
my chest heaving.

What if I let Cass find me in the dark?

What if I wasn't afraid?

19

Barbara

Venice, Italy
1635

Neither of us move

Neither of us speak.

A single word
could break the bubble around us.

Shatter
all the windows.

He walks toward me,
reaches for my hand.

Brushes his lips across
the inside of my palm.

With his eyes closed
he slides
my hand
across his rough cheeks,
kisses the inside
of my wrist,
and looks at me.

Waits for me.

I can hear the music
of my heart
pumping blood
into every vein,
my breath
the tingle
as I stand,
pulsing.

He moves closer
like a man
in the forest
not wanting to spook
a deer.

Gently
the tips of his fingers
draw the line
of my cheeks
and jaw.

His lips find mine.

He dips his body
deep into me,
pushing his lower half
in between my legs,
and lifts me
inches from the floor.

I feel his body's beat
one deep kiss at a time.

He carries me to
the small bed,
barely big enough for the two of us.

I feel his full weight
on top of me, his breath
jagged
as he runs his hands
down my dress.
I moan as he grasps my thigh
and wraps it around his waist.

He presses
into the layers of my skirts
and wails
a frustrated sigh.

Jumps from the bed.

   You need to leave!

What?
Nicolò, I don't understand.

   I can't . . .

I stand up.

Awkwardly adjust
my dress,
my hair.

I feel dizzy.
My lower half aches,
and wants that
deep press
again.

It's okay, Nicolò

    No. It's not.

I want you.

    No. You don't.
    Not really.

Yes, I do.

I don't care
if we can't get married.

I don't care
if you can't offer me anything.

    You don't understand.

    I can't have you.

    I don't have the right.

My chest seizes.
My hands clench.

You're not listening.

I don't care if we're married.

You have the right,
if I give you the right.

    No, Barbara.

    I don't.

    You can't.

Why?

    Because there are plans.

My body turns
ice cold.

    What plans?

        I wanted to tell you

        I tried to tell you.

        *But I didn't want
to hurt you.*

Nicolò walks around the room,
running his hands through his hair.

He looks like he's trapped
in a snare.

    It's Strozzi.

Strozzi?

    And your mother.

20

Lula

Venice, Italy
2025

Disoriented

Blinking, blinded, like a deep-sea life-form
that has finally been exposed to light,
I stumble out of the exhibit
and walk straight into a work zone.

I kick a bucket.
Slip on drop cloths that are strewn across the floor.

A man jumps off a ladder and runs to my aide.
My ankle hurts, and I feel dizzy.
Luciana?
I lift my head.
I'm nose-to-nose with the boy from the opera.
Vico? I say, unsure if it's him.

I knew we would see each other again!
He hugs me, lifts me, returns me to the ground,
and looks deep into my eyes.

I straighten my back, and dust off my pants,
still trying to get my balance.

What are you doing now? he says,
peeling off a white restoration coat,
wiping his hands on a cloth.

I'm heading to the Palazzo Grimani.
I have to meet my group.

As soon as I mention them,
I think of Cass and blush.

Vico closes a few opened jars
filled with distilled water,
something that looks like white paste,
and gathers his materials onto a cart.
I'll walk with you.

Aren't you working? I ask.
I stare at the scenic fresco in front of us.

Several women playing musical instruments
on the steps of a temple.

The bottom left corner
where he has been cleaning
looks more vibrant than the rest.

It's time for a break.
He hangs a sign on the cart that says, *Attenzione!*

That would have been useful a moment ago, I say, and smirk.

Then we wouldn't have run into each other,
he says, flashing a dashing smile.

My knees feel wobbly.

I shield my eyes from the sun

Vico takes my hand and smiles shyly.

Walks with me through a maze of streets.

We come to a T in the road.

We must choose.

Right or left.

There's graffiti in front of us.

DEVI PASSARE ATTRAVERSO LA PORTA DI SALICE

It's a picture of a tree with branches
that reach to the sky.

Roots under the earth.

A spiral in between.

I read the writing on the wall

Devi passare attraverso la porta di salice.

Vico laughs. *You're so cute when you speak my language.*
I crinkle my nose and scowl. *What does it mean?*

He translates slowly, pointing to each word.
You must pass through the willow tree.

I like the design, he says.
There's a community of artists.
They leave things like this.

Perhaps graffiti is like contemporary frescoes,
he says, and chuckles.

I place my cheek on the painted spiral.
Feel the heat, smell the salt.

I push.

Nothing moves.

Vico takes my hand and starts walking away.

I turn back.
I can't stop staring at the spiral.

At the Campo Santa Maria Formosa

I admire the white building,
with three tiered columns, leading to a balcony,
overlooking the square.

The Palazzo Ruzzini,
I say to Vico.

Home of the great Loredano,
and the Academy of the Unknowns.

Barbara Strozzi, the woman I'm studying,
gave many concerts here.

He listens and says,
I know this hotel, but I do not know
about this woman.

I hold his gaze.
She joined the academy meetings.
Sang and played for them.
Led their discussions.
They called her a siren.
The new Sappho.
La virtuosissima cantatrice.

And yet . . .

I stop talking and turn my back to Vico.

I'm filled with a strange melancholy.

I stare at the balcony and shiver.

I don't know why, but I see someone leaning
far over the edge, trying not to fall.

20

Barbara

Venice, Italy
1635

They are offering you

   to the highest bidder.

My eyes
don't leave his.

Ice runs through my veins.

I feel like I have swallowed
blue poison.

Offering what, exactly?

   Your maidenhood.

My body?

   There's to be a flower ceremony.

   You are to give a red rose
   to the champion.

   And Loredano,
   with all his wealth,
   and command,
   and pride . . .

   has won.

My body has been sold.
Like fish at the market.

To the iciest,
the coldest
buyer.

> *They don't know who won.*

> *Not until the ceremony.*

> *But I do.*

His voice breaks.

> *They made me count the money.*

I have been
laid out
on a frozen bed.

Gutted
for all to see.

> *I wanted so badly
> to be your champion.*

> *To save you.*

> *From what's to come.*

He's crying now.

His face
collapsed into itself.

He sits on the edge
of his small bed,
in his one room
covered in books
and music
and art.

A single
minute anchovy
swimming in an ocean
of sharks.

I run out of the room

down the stairs
through the alley
until I can find a breakthrough
to the canal.

I collapse onto all fours.

Suck the salt
air through my nostrils.

Weeping and praying
to a God
I want to believe in.

I march back to the apartment

Up the stairs
straight through the door.

Nicolò
looks up, startled.

Wearing nothing
but his linen shorts.

His eyes are wild
and scared.

His chest is bare.

*I will not give myself
to the highest bidder.*

*I will give myself
to whomever I choose.*

My fingers fumble
against my dress laces.
I tear and pull
at the ties.

Until I am down
to my linens.

We stare at each other.

His wide eyes
roam across my bare skin.

You don't understand.

Yes. I do.

This will ruin you.

Your chances.
Your future.

I walk toward him
and unlace
my under-dress.

It turns out I am betting
as well.

On who?

I pull the dress over my shoulders
and stand before him
naked
glowing
in the moonlight.

On myself.

(CHORUS)

Magic:

rock walls

bridges

paths that lead you in

then out

you think

you have found the way

but then

you are back

in the beginning

the twisted circle

search within

the walls covered

in paint and vines

the water, dreams

you will

find the center

there is beauty here

more beauty

than one heart

can hold

21

Lula

Venice, Italy
2025

We walk to the edge

of the square, pass over a bridge, and finally find
the entrance of the Palazzo Grimani.

Home of the Scuola di Musica Antica di Venezia,
the Venice School of Early Music.

I hesitate at the door.
We have to say goodbye here.

Vico's lips droop, and he pouts.
We still have so much to see.

I smile and say, *This was a lovely walk.*
Thank you for everything.

He touches my shoulder.
I want more days.

I give him *un bacetto.*
A kiss on the right cheek, then the left.

He's so good-looking.
It's intoxicating. Breathtaking.

I want to spend day after day
talking about art and architecture,
but I have a sinking feeling in my stomach.

I have work to do.
I need to focus on my music, my life,
my friends.

Healing.

At least tell me where you're staying, he pleads.
Takes my hand in both of his hands.

Hotel Giorgione, I say.

He walks backward, blowing kisses in the air.

Turns and shouts, *Che bella! Luciana!*
into the crowded square.

The courtyard is buzzing with excitement

Music students and directors
carrying violins, cellos, horns, fill the space,
shout out, bob, and weave
like water taxi drivers vying for space
on the Grand Canal.

My heart lunges when I see Cass across the courtyard.
His lute case slung over his shoulder.
He's grinning as he introduces himself to other groups.
I see the girls swooning over his golden eyes.

My stomach tightens with jealousy.

I search the crowd, and see Agatha
jumping up and down, waving her arms.
I was getting worried, she shouts.

I hug her tightly.
I'm fine.

She holds me at arm's distance.
You look different.

What do you mean? I give her a confused smile.

You look ravishing and, dare I say, confident.
You're oozing sensuality. Wait!
Did you meet up with that smoke show from the opera?

I snort. *How did you know?*
Agatha squeals, *I can always detect an aroma of romance!*

I had a good day, but I really missed being with you all.

Agatha squeezes me. *We missed you too,*
but I'm psyched you had a romantic rendezvous!
He is absolutely GORGEOUS!

Cass sneaks up from behind,
sticks his face between us, wiggles his eyebrows,
and says, *Are you talking about me AGAIN?*

I give him a smirk.
Yes. Cass. I can't stop thinking about you.

For a moment I think I'm joking.

But as the words flow from my lips,
I know I'm telling the truth.

Jenkins gathers us together

I really want you to see this ensemble from Venezuela.
They have a male soprano. Everyone has been talking about him
since his stage debut at a Handel festival in Germany last year.

Madison raises her hand. *You mean a countertenor?*
No, Madison, Jenkins says, *I do not mean a countertenor.*

Countertenors use their falsetto, which lacks any chest resonance.
Male sopranos use their chest voice all the way up to the top
of their register, similar to a tenor. They just have thin enough
vocal folds to pull it off.

She raises her eyebrows and says,
He can support a high D.

My eyes bulge.
What?! I say. *I can only sing a high C.*
That's why he's so incredible, Jenkins says.

She makes sure everyone is looking.
I thought this might be a good time to talk
about the role of the "castrato," or the plural "castrati,"
during this period that we're studying.
Can anyone tell me what they know about the castrati?

Brick scoffs and chimes in,
Dude! Aren't those the dudes with no nuts?
Jenkins's face holds steady, while the rest of us erupt.
She looks him directly in the eye, with lips as flat
as a loosely tuned string, and says, *Anyone else?*

Agatha raises her hand and says,
Doesn't "castrati" mean "castrated"?

Jenkins nods.
Yes. It was a church-sanctioned procedure they gave boys
with promising voices, between the ages of six and eight.
Many of them were castrated and never became successful,
but those who did were worshipped and became gloriously wealthy.

Agatha grabs her chest.
How brutal.

Jenkins places her hand on Agatha's shoulders.
The procedure became illegal around the turn of the century.
I wanted to talk about this for several reasons.
First, because I was thinking while we were watching L'Orfeo
that most of the original actors in that production
playing female roles would have been castrati.
They would not have let female actors perform.

It's not until the late seventeenth century that we see the first
opera performances by women. And second, I wanted you
to see this remarkable singer today, so that we can see
a modern example of what's possible, without surgery.

We walk through the three-story whitewashed
courtyard, up the stairs to a long hall filled with chairs
that lead to a stage.

The director of the school opens his arms

Welcome to the splendid Palazzo Grimani!

*A glorious space for music from an architectural
and acoustic point of view, but it is also a place
that has had crucial importance for the history of music.*

*The Grimani family were among the first in the seventeenth century
to dedicate a theater to public opera,
the SS. Giovanni e Paolo, and later built the most sumptuous
of Venetian theaters, the S. Giovanni Grisostomo.*

*They were therefore in contact with all the major musicians
of the time. Among the most famous:
Monteverdi, Cavalli, and Handel.*

*We hope you will feel the spirit of this notorious,
noble family and remember the musicians
throughout history who have blessed these halls with their voices,
as we listen to the most remarkable and accomplished
ensembles from across the world.*

Arturo Herrera

stands on the stage, tight white silk pants
and vest, platform heels, and a matching organza cape
cascading around him. He holds his hands out,
gesturing with each lilt of his voice
as he sings Handel's "Care selve."
I close my eyes and imagine it's the famous castrato
Farinelli singing, so agile and clear.
He flashes his white teeth,
his fingers flutter through the air as if on a keyboard,
he cups his hands around his ears to feel the trills.
The lightness, the power, thrills me.

After the performance

Jenkins gathers the group.
We need to pick out your instruments. Agatha claps her hands.
The director of the school leads us to a storage space.
Whoa, we all say in unison.
Ancient instruments fill the room,
grand pieces that should be in a museum.

*Of course, we cannot allow you to use
some of the more valuable pieces, but you can pick among these.*
He points to two sculpted and gilded harps.
Agatha's jaw is open, her eyes wide with delight.
She takes a small stool and tries one.
Her fingers cascading along the strings
sound like delicate drops of dew pooling
on open flower petals.

She shifts the stool to the other harp,
leans the soundboard on her shoulder, and plays again.
This feels more natural. It fits my frame a little better.

Cass tries a theorbo. He plucks the gut strings
on the long neck that extends twice the normal reach of a lute.
It looks like a construction crane, Brick says, and for once he's right.

Cass plays a little Bach, and then follows it up with the first lick
of "Seven Nation Army" by the White Stripes.
This is sick!

Jenkins laughs and points to the extended neck.
Listen to that depth of sound, the sheer tonal weight.
It's incredible, says Cass, who starts to play Bartolotti.

Cynthe opens her mouth, makes a squeaking noise,
and then closes it.
Cynthe? Jenkins asks. *Do you have a question?*

She clears her throat.
I'm wondering . . . if I could try . . . one of the harpsichords?

The director smiles. *Of course!*
I have something special, something rare.
You cannot use this in the performance. We cannot move it.
But because I am here with you, you can try it.

Professor Jenkins told me that one of you
is studying Barbara Strozzi. . . .
I blush and raise my hand. Professor Jenkins beams.

Well . . . I have a theory that this may have been
Giulio Strozzi's harpsichord.
It's only a guess, based on ownership records,
but I love the idea that this may have been used
to create the lyrics for some of the first operas performed in Venice.

Cynthe walks to an instrument painted with blues
and greens, a pastoral scene, clouds and ocean shoreline.

A siren holds the carved supporting beams.

I place my hand on the polished lid,
and a shiver runs up my spine.

It feels like it holds years of music.

Cynthe lifts the lid, and we all gasp, noticing that the painting
continues underneath. *How gorgeous,* Jenkins whispers.
Her voice filled with reverence.

Cynthe plays a few phrases of Monteverdi,
and we hear the brittle, rattling uniform timbre
of the plucked strings.

And look at this. The director runs his finger
along the edge. *I want to show you what's here, under the lid.*

He puts on his glasses to read the script.
Cuore in fiamme. La chiave scivola tra le dita, he says slowly.
Heart on fire. The key slides through your fingers.

He takes off his glasses. Madison leans in and asks,
What is that supposed to mean?

I roll my eyes.
Even when she's excited, she sounds bitchy.

The director shrugs.
Perhaps they are talking about a harpsichord key?
Baroque libertines loved to obfuscate their meaning.
They layered their visual art and music with hidden codes.

Jenkins offers, *Maybe they're saying*
that your heart is on fire when you're playing music.
I know mine is. I smile at her.

Our elegant, empowering leader.
I hope someday I can be just like her.
Lit by a fire always shining
through my voice, my heart.

Jenkins addresses the group.
You have a free evening, and then we'll rendezvous
early in the morning for practice. Nine a.m. in the lobby.
Don't be late!

She makes special eye contact
with Brick, who mouths, *Who, me?*

Before we separate, she joins me and asks,
How are you feeling, Lula?

I want to tell her

the feeling of music
and humming and happiness is alive
in my body again.
I want to tell her that the salty air in Venice
makes my throat feel open,
and the crowds and the smells and the cats
and the alleyways don't make me feel lost,
or claustrophobic.
They make me feel strangely at home.
Closer to my friends and community.
I want to say, When I'm here,
I am also someplace else. I am shifting in and out
of the years, the footprints, the history,
the people who wandered aimlessly through this labyrinth,
loving and fighting, creating art.
I can feel the shadows and the ghosts, the music,
the silence, the plague victims buried beneath
the streets, the bells that have rung in the towers for years
after endless years, the swish of long skirts
against the cobblestone, the click of heels,
see the frames of boats being built in the harbor,
the howling of the accused, crossing the Bridge of Sighs,
shielded faces behind masks, the passion of lips,
the grasping of one body against another,
and I feel all of it in my mind, my heart,
the carnival of time, swirling like a drop of blood in water.
But I can't. I can't explain.
So, I look and her, and smile. I say, *I'm fine.*
I'm doing just fine.

21

Barbara

Venice, Italy
1635

I storm up the stairs

through the hallway,
into the parlor.

Signore is sitting on the couch.

My mother resting
on his lap,
a perched pet.

They look startled,
yet happy.

Ché cose, ragazza brillante?

Signore beams at me.

How could you?

What are you talking about, bella?

How could you sell me?

To the highest bidder?

Like a house or a boat?
Or an ANIMAL!

My mother is by my side.

Nicolò told me.
You can't deny it!

We were trying to protect you.

Protect me?
You were just trying to make money
for yourselves!
You are selfish!
And cruel!

No, Barbara.

This was all for you.

Is this why you gave me my own room?

So I could be taken?
Behind closed doors?
While you counted your gold?

I clench my fists and scream.
In frustration.
In rage.

I turn to signore.
Point a finger in his face.

You.
You know how vicious
these men can be.

How could you do this?
To your own daughter!

> *My daughter?*
> *I'm sorry, Barbara.*
> *I think you have misunderstood.*
> *I am not . . .*

His eyes are frantic.

Jutting and spinning in their sockets.

He is drowning,
looking for a raft.

No one is coming to save him.

> *You are not my daughter.*

What are you talking about?
Of course I am!

> *You do not have my name.*

You and my mother
have been sleeping in the same room
since I was a baby.

I know I'm your daughter.
Just tell me!

> *It is not my story to tell!*

I look at my mother.

She covers her face
with her hands
and begins to weep.

22
Lula

Venice, Italy
2025

I pull Agatha toward the vendors

in the Campo Santa Maria Formosa.
Look at all of this.

Stacks of dusty books, boxes of antique coins,
intermixed with religious pendants, lockets,
framed black-and-white photographs,
pottery, and chipped china.

Agatha picks up a carnival mask and holds it up to her face.
The long, beaked nose of a plague doctor
makes goose bumps rise on my neck.

I think we've had enough plague, I say,
remembering the years of wearing black masks.
Public places packed with uniformly covered faces,
sad eyes, living through the trauma
of a pandemic—together, yet alone.

Agreed, says Agatha,
and places the mask back on the table.
I shuffle through loose pages, pictures,
and maps torn from old books.

The woman behind the table stares at my ring
as I reach for an antique coin.
She looks me in the eyes,
and pulls out a wooden box.
She opens it, and I see that it's filled with skeleton keys.

I spy one that's especially large and brass,
with an intricate filigree handle.
My heart jumps.
I pull it from the box and admire it.
It's connected to a long, delicate chain.
I thought you might like that one,
the woman says with a smile, and closes the box.
I place the chain around my neck.

Agatha grabs a flowing yellow scarf
and wraps it around her neck,
admiring herself in a hand mirror.

Do you really need another scarf? I ask.
A woman can never have too many scarves, she says,
and hands the woman a two-euro coin.

How much for this? I ask the vendor,
motioning to my new necklace.

It's a gift, she says.

Thank you, I say, feeling honored.

She smiles and adds,
There's going to be a storm tonight.
Acqua alta, *the rising tide.*
It happens quickly.
There might be flooding in the square.
Be safe.

She places her palms together,
lifts them to her forehead, then to her heart,
and then bows.

May the mother always be with you.

22
Barbara

Venice, Italy
1635

I should have told you long ago

My mother is weeping.

Hiding behind her hands.

> *I was afraid you would*
> *hate me*
> *disrespect me*
> *loathe me.*
>
> *I was afraid you would know*
> *how damaged, how afraid*
> *how ruined*
> *I was.*
>
> *Please don't be angry with signore.*
> *It's not his fault.*
>
> *All he has ever done*
> *is save me.*
>
> *Save us.*
> *Over and over again.*

Signore begins to weep.

He holds
my mother's hand to his cheek
and whispers,

> *Madonna,*
> *you have done the same for me.*
>
> *You have turned a lonely, cynical poet*
> *into a loved man.*

He kisses her.

I see their love for the first time.

There is a part of me that melts,
wants to rejoice,
to know the truth.

But I can't.
They have sold me.

My parents died when I was young

My mother speaks softly.

> *I had nothing.*
> *No one would hire me.*

> *Or marry me.*

> *I was a street urchin.*
> *A beggar.*

> *Stealing bread and apples*
> *at the market.*

> *Madame Carmina*
> *found me.*

> *She taught me*
> *the art*
> *of how to be a courtesan.*

She has avoided my eyes
until now.

Her gaze is hard
and pointed.

> *I became one of the best.*

She beams
with a glimmer of pride.

> *And then one night*
> *I encountered something*
> *I couldn't handle.*

> *Several men together.*

They wanted violence.
They wanted to hurt me.

When I tried to fight them,
they set a fire.

I was left.
In a ditch.
Beaten. Burned.

Unable to do my job.

Left with these.

She unlaces her bodice,
and I see the scars
I have known all my life
along her chest
and breast
and stomach.

She points to the gash
across her lip.

Madame Carmina
said I was no use to her.

She threw me out
onto the street
again.

Soon after,
I found out I was pregnant
with you.

My mother
brushes her hand against my cheek.
I shrug her away.

> *What was I to do?*
> *I could barely feed myself.*
>
> *I took you*
> *to deposit you at the* ospedale.
>
> *The* scafetta.
>
> *I stood there in front of the window.*
> *Weeping.*
>
> *My child. My daughter.*
> *I could not leave you.*

I look at the floor.
Try not to cry.

Her words echo
in my ears.

> Signore
> saved me from the gutter.
>
> *He gave me a job.*
> *Gave us a life.*
>
> *We would have nothing*
> *without his kindness.*

I look at signore,
but he is looking at my mother.

Tears streaming down his face.

My mother
looks at me again.

I never had what you have.

Real talent.

I close my eyes
as she takes my hands
in hers.

*You have something that men
admire.*

They see your strength.

*Your tenderness, your intellect
when you sing.*

*You have the chance
to be great, Barbara.*

Better than I ever was.

My eyes burn with tears.

Take their money, Barbara.
Become a powerful courtesan.

Listen to them.
Soothe them.

Hear their stories and their secrets.
Use this to gain even more power.

I don't want power.
I want my freedom.

You and I know.
*There is no freedom
for women like us.*

I want to make music.
I want to write and compose.

You can.

They will pay you as a courtesan to sing for them.
Pleasure them.

I want to be independent.

You will have money of your own.

Save your money for a dowry.

I have seen courtesans do this.
They can marry any man they wish.

Many men will want you.
They will beg for you.

I want to live with you.
In our own house.
Like we've always wanted.

I will never leave you.

I will help you
to raise your family.

If I sell myself...
I look her in the eye.
If you sell me,
I will never be anything
but a whore.

My voice breaks.

My mother stands
and takes me in her arms.

Her embrace
tightens,
a vine
encircling a tree.

*I say this
not as your mother
but as a woman who has struggled
to find her place in a world
designed by men.*

*I am giving you a way
to have your freedom,
and your music.*

*If you do this ceremony,
you will have choices.*

*Without it,
you have nothing.*

23

Lula

**Venice, Italy
2025**

We gather at Palazzo Grimani to practice

Run through all the different pieces.
I'm in awe of how amazing everyone sounds,
when Jenkins turns to me.
Lula, would you like to try to sing "Che si può fare"?
My throat clenches, and my stomach turns.
All I can do is shake my head. *No.*

Her eyes soften, but she places her fingers on her temples.
I guess we'll have to go with "What Can We Poor Females Do?"
Everyone except Brick and Madison groans.
Jenkins says to the group, *I'm not sure we have anything else.*

Brick adds, *I think it's going to be quite humorous. You'll see!*
Madison thumps Brick on the back and tries to smile.
It will be great, honey.

Jenkins clears her throat, throws her fist into the air
in a pitiful cheer. *Two more days!*
She looks around for support.
Yay! Cass tries his hardest,
but even his unending enthusiasm is waning.

Jenkins straightens her spine. *You have all worked
so hard. No matter what songs we sing,
the audience will see your talent. This is going to work!*

I know this is all my fault. They're all counting
on me, and I'm letting them down.

On our way home

we turn a corner.
I see a young woman walking toward me.
Striking blue eyes and long braided hair.
I stare at the black writing on the front
of her white T-shirt.
 PE:I:TI:A
She looks at me, and we make eye contact.
She smiles and places her palms together,
then places them at her heart.

She reminds me of the woman
with sapphire eyes in Boston.

The symbol of the goddess.

The resonance of the crystal bowls
fills my ears.

We round the corner

My stomach flips.

Vico is seated at the café in front of our hotel.
I see him before he sees me.

He's drinking an espresso and reading a paperback.
His hair has fallen over his eyes.
He's wearing khakis and a crisp white T-shirt,
white Converse sneakers. He stands up when he sees me.
His eyes brighten. His excitement makes my chest feel tight.
Ciao, bella Luciana.

His blond hair falls over one eye.
He tucks his paperback into his back pocket and smiles shyly.
I couldn't wait to see you again.

I whisper to Cass and Agatha, *I'll see you in there.*
Cass glares at me. I physically angle his body
toward the hotel, give him a push, then join Vico at the café.

Vico orders me an Aperol Spritz,
and it arrives orange and glowing,
with green olives, and a bowl of potato chips.

The evening sun makes everything look like a photograph.
The salt and sweet and bitter warm my insides.

We talk for a moment about subjects as light
as the ice floating in my drink.

I do not tell him about the attack,
my inability to perform.

My shame.

I take another sip,
close my eyes, and savor this moment.

I look at Vico.

He makes me feel like an actress in a movie
about finding romance, travel, love, adventure.

But he's the wrong leading man.

Vico walks me to the hotel entrance

Moves forward to kiss me.
I turn away from him.

He presses his lips to my cheek.

Cass is standing in the lobby,
waiting for me.

I have to go, I say to Vico.
Tomorrow? he says.

Maybe, I respond,
*but I'm in Venice for the festival,
and I'm going to be really busy.*

He drops his head.
I know he understands the words
that I'm not saying.

I start to turn, and he pulls me back.
There's a storm coming.

He looks at the sky.
*Strong south wind means rising tide.
The town is preparing for flooding.
Be careful tonight.*

He kisses me again on the cheek.
Goodbye, Luciana.

As I walk toward Cass,
I see Agatha and Cynthe
waiting behind him
with stern expressions.

Their arms are crossed.

23

Barbara

Venice, Italy
1635

Come with me

My mother takes my hand.

Where are you taking me?

We descend the stairs
and head for the front door.

Where are we going?

You'll see.

She's gaining energy with each step.

Weaving quickly through the alleyways.

I don't want to follow her.
I don't trust her.

She pulls me along
like a dinghy on a rope
in shallow water.

Along the canal,
around bends, and bridges,
and shadowed corners.

Until we arrive at a brick wall,
with a rectangular mosaic pattern.

She pushes on one of the bricks,
and I gasp.

A hidden door creaks open
into a courtyard,
full of vines and statues,
a pool of water
that connects to the canal.

We walk
to an arched entrance.

What is this place?
I ask
as I run my hand
over the carving on the door.

One of my many secrets,
she says with a wink.

My mother lifts her hand,
inserts a key,
and twists.

The door opens.

We enter a cold gray hallway

I smell the ancient rock,
the cavernous
emptiness.

I want to run.
I want to scream.

I want to trust my mother,
but I cannot.

Not after
what she has done.

I long for it to be
just her and me once more.

Tucked into the attic.

Mother and daughter
against the world.

Warmth
against the cold.

At the end of the vestibule

there are two towering doors
carved with a tree.

Bare branches
sprawled across a night sky,
inlaid with
mother-of-pearl stars.

My mother swings wide
the doors.

What lies on the other side
takes my breath away.

A massive
two-story room
covered in scrolled wooden shelves
carved with crescents
and crests.

A ceiling swirling
with opalescent clouds
and birds
and the sun moving across the sky
from the orange-yellow haze
of rising
to the purple gray of dusk.

The space
is as big and as hushed
as a cathedral.

It is a church.
Filled with books.

What is this place?

Do you like it?

*It's the most beautiful place
I've ever seen.*

What is it called?

A library.

Who do all these books belong to?

You and me.

I walk to the stacks

Run my hands
over the leather and gold spines.

Titles in Italian
and languages I don't recognize.

Fairy tales, novels,
science, maps.

> *It's one of the benefits*
> *of being a courtesan.*

> *We are not bound to the rules of society.*

> *We can educate ourselves.*

She opens my palm
and places the key
in the center of my hand
and closes my fingers.

I feel the cool weight
of the gold.

Brush my thumb
against the splendid
carved design.

> *This is yours now.*
> *You belong here.*

I look across the room

to the staircase.
Women who look like nuns,
wearing red habits,
wander the second floor.

One meets our gaze,
folds her hands in prayer,
touches them to her forehead
and her heart,
and silently bows.

Who are they?

> *They are the keepers of the books.*

> *An order of women*
> *who have been here for generations,*
> *long before I came.*

Are they courtesans?

> *They are dedicated*
> *to the protection of this place.*

> *And all the women*
> *who find their way here.*

> *Women*
> *who seek knowledge.*

> *And healing.*

Her eyes focus on mine

*Loredano's men
call themselves
the Academy of the Unknowns.*

But they are not unknown.

We are.

I look around
at the women here.

The keepers of the books.

Their red dresses and veils,
their diamond-shaped belts.

Guardians of history.

For those
whose stories
have never been told.

I forgive her

For her scheming.
For her manipulation.
For her past.
For her secrets.

Like mother,
like daughter.

I have secrets too.

(CHORUS)

Mirror:

glass

that reflects

and glass

that bends

shadows

and light

blur

and distend

stare into

the blue

another soul

stares back

at you

24
Lula

Venice, Italy
2025

What is this? An intervention?

I say with a nervous hiccup.
What are you doing?! Cass says in an accusing tone.
What are you talking about? I look at him, unflinching.

Cass motions to Vico walking away.
With Signor Smooth!
He spits the words at me.
Agatha puts a hand on his shoulder.

Cass motions to Agatha and Cynthe.
We've been worried about you for weeks!
Protecting you. Making sure you're okay.
Now you're off, wandering the city alone,
drinking with some guy
who knows nothing about you!

I glare at him. *Maybe that's why*
I want to spend time with him.
He's treating me like a human.
Not a trauma victim!

I raise my hands in the air.
Maybe I want what you and Agatha have!

Cass and Agatha exchange bizarre glances.
A childhood friendship? Agatha says, confused.
I don't think that's going to happen with Vico.
That takes years of band camp.

Cass laughs and then hardens his expression.

I start talking louder.
That's not what I mean, and you know it!
You two are madly in love with each other!
I stick an accusing finger in their faces.
Agatha howls.

Me? And Cass?
She looks at Cass, and they erupt into hysterical,
cascading laughter.

Cynthe breaks in with her typical deadpan.
I'm insulted.
Agatha puts her arm around Cynthe,
pulling her close. *Lula. Jesus Christ.*
I'm with Cynthe! We've been together for a month.

My jaw drops to the floor.
What?! You and Cass are always . . . all over each other.
And you and Cynthe—now I'm waving an accusing finger
between their faces—*barely touch each other.*

Cynthe, as cold as an ice bath, says,
I'm not a fan of public displays of affection.
I pause and rub my temples.
That tracks, I say.

Cynthe reaches out for Agatha's hand and says,
She really is my girlfriend.
Agatha beams. *Oh, Hyacinth! I'm blushing!*
I look at Cynthe and Agatha and crack a smile.
I have misinterpreted everything.

I—I don't know what to say,
I stammer. *I'm happy for you, but I feel bad.*
I wish I had known.
I feel like I could have supported you more.

Agatha glows and kisses me on the cheek.

I still feel confused.
I thought we talked about you and Cass.
I asked you, and you said you couldn't live
without each other.

Cass and Agatha exchange glances
and say at the same time, *We can't!*
and then start laughing again.

She lets go of Cynthe's hand and takes mine.

Lula. You are correct. Cass is head over heels in love.
She looks at Cass, and he flushes red.
His golden eyes flash.

But it's not with me.

24
Barbara

Venice, Italy
1635

My lessons are finished

with Cavalli,
but my lessons with Atto
and Nicolò
have just begun.

We spend hours dreaming

singing, playing, lounging

on Atto's living room floor.

We are supposed to be preparing
the musical entertainment
for my flower ceremony.

Or my *deflowering,*
as Atto calls it.

Instead
we drink to dizziness,
play cards, recite poetry,
stump each other with riddles,
dance and drum and shout
to the moon
and the stars.

We suck
white wine and garlic
from mussels.

Throw our heads back.
Swallow the juice.
The sea.

Our time together
is liquid gold,
olive oil,
that slicks our lips.

I do not hide my love
for Nicolò.
I sit on his lap
and rest my head in the crook of his neck.

I seek his mouth
with fruit and kisses.

Atto claps hands
and twirls around us,
sings love songs
about horned sheep.

And gods
who turn themselves
into clouds
of gold
and fall in love
with mortal maidens.

He encourages us
to be ourselves,
share our love
in the open.

Cast aside the notion
of patriarchal permission
and societal expectation.

Which Atto does often
with Bruno.

Who has become
a trusted friend too.

This is the only place
where I feel safe.

Our friendship
held sacred.

Our secrets kept.

On rare days

Atto does not come
to the door.

Bruno kisses our cheeks
and shakes his head.

Not today.

This is not a good day.

The lock clicks.

None of us who dare

to create
and feel
and yearn

who dare open
ourselves,
vulnerable
to the world

who dare challenge
the rules
society has set
for us

who dare pursue
a passionate
honest
life

who dare
to love
and be loved

none of us,
even though we try
to provide
each other home and harbor,

none of us who dare
are safe.

(CHORUS)

Bells:

there is no more time to waste

there is music

movement

a call to action

we have been watching

up here in this tower

years of longing

memory

we see you

hear us

it is time

25

Lula

Venice, Italy
2025

It starts to rain

I stare at Cass.
His golden eyes shoot arrows into my chest.
I—I— I stammer, and start to back away.
I don't know what to say.
I don't know what to do.
I need time to think.
I back through the open door.
It's raining hard, and my shoes slip on the stones
as I turn down the alley.

I just had a drink with a charming Italian,
who loves history and art,
who is gorgeous and wants to kiss me.

But. He's not Cass.

Lula! I open my eyes.
Cass has followed me.
He's soaking wet.
Trying to wipe the water from his eyes.
Lula. Please, stop. Look at me.

I keep walking. I can't stop.
I take a left, and then a right. I need a quiet spot.
He's close behind.

He keeps talking. *I know this is a surprise.*
I should have told you, but I was afraid
you wouldn't feel the same way.
I was afraid my feelings would ruin our friendship.
You were hurt. You were healing.

I turn another corner, into a private alleyway
with an arched portico, leading to a courtyard.
I didn't want to make you feel unsafe.

I look behind me,
at beautiful, loving Cass.

His olive skin glowing in the lamplight.

The water is pooling at our feet.
The tide is rising,
onto the concrete, from the canal.
Acqua alta.

I pull him into the courtyard.

Cass . . . , I say, and stop.
I search for his eyes,
as he stammers, *It's—it's okay, Lula.*
Staying friends is good. It's important.
It's enough.

I put my finger to his lips.
Cass. He stops talking.
I can hear his breathing.

Cass. I want you. I've always wanted you.

Without words

he leans me against the wall. I can smell the moisture,
the dirt, the ancient, packed bricks. Taste the salt. The rain.
He places his hands on my face, his lips to my lips.
Until I forget all the pain and melt into a blur of indigo,
evening haze, the sound of the swallows pulsing in the air,
the lapping of the waves at the mouth, the entrance, the steps.
Late afternoon light on the lead glass circles of the windows.
The water. Our lips meet again and again. I smell and taste him.
I want him. All of him. More than I've ever wanted anyone in my life.
Surrounded by shine and shadow. Is this what love feels like?
Forgiving. Immediate. Devoted. Adoring. Insistent.

I pull away

His grin is hilarious.
I knew this was going to happen.

I punch him on the shoulder.
No you didn't.
Yes. I did.
I'm grinning now, and laughing
as I say, *Can we do it again?*

He grabs me and pulls me to him,
tight and rough, in a playful way.

Oh, I'm not going to stop doing this.
He kisses me on the cheek.
Breakfast. Kiss. *Lunch.* Kiss.
And dinner.

His kisses me again on the lips.

So deep and sensual,
it makes my spine straighten,
and my toes curl under.

I look around the courtyard

I see red flowers growing in window boxes,
bright against the gray.

I gasp. *Oh my God, Cass.*
We're at Barbara's house.

What? he asks, standing by my side.

I walk to the steps leading to a carved door.

The rain is pelting down on us.
The water is rising,
covering our shoes.
Lula, we should go. This is getting bad,
Cass says, looking around
at the flooded courtyard.

I place my hand on the pewter handle,
my cheek to the marble doorframe.

Home, I say to myself.

The wind picks up and whips
my hair around my face.
I feel my body jolt with the power
and force of it.

I can see the children running in the courtyard,
the laundry hanging to dry.

I can hear the laughter, the singing.

I can feel her.

25

Barbara

Venice, Italy
1635

Atto and I travel

on a gondola
to Ca' Sagredo
in matching attire.

Red corseted frocks
that don't leave much
to the imagination.

Atto's stubble
and tufts of chest hair
powdered white
and accented with lace.

Pearls drip from our necks
and ears.
We chime together
as we move and laugh.

Nicolò blesses us
with his honeyed lute.

One foot up on the side,
he looks like a
drunken troubadour
as he bounces his full voice
off the brick walls
that line the narrow canal.

Bruno at our feet
covers, then exposes us
with a giant white ostrich fan
in a frolicking game
of peekaboo.

I am giggling
uncontrollably.

We've never been more ourselves.

Sweet, drunken fun ends

as we arrive
at the cavernous entrance.

Cherry-red and indigo
Ottoman rugs
line the hallways.

A steward ushers us
up the stairs
to the *portego*,
a long,
forest-green salon
that runs the length of the first floor.

Chandeliers
made of Murano glass
drip
from the ceiling.

At the end of the hall,
the light
from the Grand Canal
filters through
the mosaic panes
of the arched windows.

The sun wavers
and swirls,
mimics the waves
of the lagoon
below.

I admire
the painted scene
of Pyramus and Thisbe.

Star-crossed lovers
who whispered
their love for each other
through a crack
in the wall
between their two divided
households.

I spy my mother
searching for me in the crowd.

Nicolò drops my hand,
and falls behind.

I enter
the golden ballroom
with Atto
by my side.

Ferrante blocks our way

Ah! Atto!
Always playing a role.

Tonight I see you have chosen
the damsel in distress.

Atto flicks a fan,
pulls petticoats into a curtsy,
looks toward Ferrante.
Flutters eyelashes
and says,

> *It turns out the role of the evil villain*
> *was already taken.*

Ferrante hisses
through his teeth,

> *If you're going to have all the privileges*
> *of a man,*
> *perhaps you should act like one.*

Loredano stands next to Ferrante.

Laughs
and sighs
as he takes Atto's
hand and kisses it.

> *Ferrante!*

> *You're just jealous that*
> *Atto ignores all your many advances.*

> *And prefers . . .*
> *a manservant.*

Atto howls with joy.

    My dear Loredano!

    How dashing!

    I do believe you've never been
    so attractive
    as you are right now.

Ferrante's eyes fill with fire.

He reaches out,
gives a brutal tug,
and rips Atto's corset.

    I guess you're not ready
    for the stage
    after all.

Atto gasps,
reaches for the laces
to heal the gash,
the wound.

I rush to Atto's side.

Stop it, Ferrante!

    This isn't your concern,
    bastarda.

Atto turns to leave.
I rush to follow.

Looking back,
throwing daggers
out of my eyes
into Ferrante's heart.

I find Atto in a closet

trying to fix the costume.

I gather Atto
to my chest
with fierce loyalty.

Pull a hairpin
and a ribbon from my hair,
help to lace
the corset
back together.

I wipe the tears
as Atto whispers,

> *We used to be a thing,*
> *you know.*

> *Me and Ferrante.*

Atto laughs.

> *He was uncharacteristically kind.*

> *Until he wasn't.*

> *Then I realized he was a sea slug.*

I let out a snort
as I stitch the fabric.

> *He's more vicious than that!*

> *A scorpion fish?*

Atto grabs my hand,
becoming more serious.

> *He's dangerous, Barbara.*
> *I mean it.*

I continue with my work.

I know he is.

Atto is silent,
then takes a big breath.

Eyes filled with tears.

> *I was eight years old.*
>
> *When they cut me.*

Atto...

I stop mending.

I place my hands
on Atto's shoulders
and make eye contact.

> *They carried me out of bed one morning,*
> *barely awake.*
>
> *It was winter.*
>
> *The bath was filled with ice*
> *from the canal.*
>
> *My parents let them.*
> *They didn't protect me.*
>
> *They thought...*
> *they were convinced...*
> *they were creating a better life for me.*

I had talent.
Everyone knew it.

They wanted to freeze me
in time.

Make me immortal.

Atto is weeping now.

I became something
I don't recognize.

The sight
of my charming, strong,
outspoken friend,
ripped and broken,
hiding in a closet,
makes me weep too.

Sometimes our parents
love us so much,
they turn us into monsters.

I grab Atto's face

*If you're a monster,
then I'm a monster too.*

Atto laughs
through tears.

Just a couple of monsters hiding in the closet.

I giggle.

*I think we deserve a little light,
don't you?*

Atto and I press our hands together

Our red hooped skirts
lean toward each other.

Let's give them a glimpse of heaven.

I send a kiss through the air.

*And then send them back to hell,
where they belong.*

We enter the music room.

Nicolò comes up behind us,
his lute pressed into his gut.

The three of us make eye contact
and take a breath
as one body.

*Nel bel fior di gioventù,
alle gioie aprire il seno.*

*In the fair flower of youth,
open your heart to joy.*

The crowd hushes
as our three voices wind together,
snakes slipping through
emerald water.

We slide
through the audience.

Men's faces upturned,
eyes closed,
necks bobbing to the rhythm.

I look at Ferrante and Loredano.

Lighting the water
with fire and oil.

*Che per comprar contenti,
non ha spaccio poi molto.*

*For in buying contentment,
you don't receive much value.*

I turn to Nicolò.

His green eyes sparkle,
starlight on the lagoon.

I turn to my mother
and bow my head.

*Bellezze fuggitive,
estinte pria che vive.*

*The beauty within you
is already fleeting even before it lives.*

The three of us arrive
at the front of the hall.

Atto on my left.
Nicolò on my right.

We sing in unison.

Alle gioie aprire il seno.

Open your heart to joy.

The crowd is silent.

Reverent.

Our voices linger in the air.

I wonder
if these are the last notes
that we will sing
together.

Applause fills the room

as Sagredo,
our host,
joins us on the stage.

He is draped in yards
of dark velvet
that billow to the floor.

Gold medallions
festoon his collar.

A voluminous white wig
accentuates
his sagging jowls.

> *We call to this temple of learning and art—*
> *the goddess Flora!*

Quivering with delight,
he places a crown of flowers
on my hair.

> *Welcome, goddess*
> *of spring and flowers and maidens!*

> *To this academy gathering*
> *at Ca' Sagredo!*

He bows to me,
and turns to the men.

> *She blossoms with youth,*
> *and beauty.*

*And like a honeybee,
bounces from flower to flower,
spreading their colorful petals,
smelling the succulent nectar,
and fertilizes our land!*

Our host points
to the two large vases
resting on the table
at our side.

Two vases

filled with many
different flowers.

The flowers
I am supposed
to give away.

To these men.
Who have paid.
For me.

These men.
Who think they can own
my innocence.

I imagine it.
Tight on the vine.
Like a fist.

My virtue,
my value,
my maidenhood.

And yet.

One bloodred rose.

In full bloom.

Blazes
in the center
of the vessel.

One rose
for the victor.

I know what is expected of me

A flower in my hand,
I walk to Sagredo.

A tulip
for wealth and prosperity.

He bows his head in thanks.

A walk to the vase
and then to Grimani.

A white lily,
for the holy virgin.

He mumbles under his breath,

> *I was hoping for a different kind of virgin.*

The men chortle
and stomp.

I reach for a flower
and walk to Nicolò.

A red carnation,
the symbol of love.

I bend down
and kiss him softly on the lips.

He looks like he's going to faint.

The men laugh
as Ferrante mumbles,

> *Save it for the winner!*

I grab a magenta orchid from the vase
and hand it to Ferrante
with lightning
on my tongue.

*An orchid
for jealousy and deceit.*

The men
fill the hall with gasps
and spasms of laughter.

Ferrante's cheeks swell,
a puffer fish
floating in the detritus.

I pluck a sprig of lavender,
and scan the room
for the most handsome man
I can find.

He's tall, standing in the back.

Bright blue eyes
smolder amid dark features
and a mop of curly
black hair.

I hand him the fragrant bloom.

Lavender for desire.

I pause for a moment,
eyes connected
with a coquettish gaze.

I pull a strawberry
off his plate,
and place it into my mouth.

He laughs aloud with pleasure.

I twirl and grasp a yellow rose
and walk to Atto.

For friendship.

Atto's eyes fill with tears,
mouth whispers,
Ti amo, my little peacock,
to make me laugh.

Finally
the moment they've all been waiting for.

The red rose
in my hand.

I walk slowly to Loredano

Stand before him.

Lean way down
until the smooth curve
of the tops
of my breasts
are right under
his nose.

Gently,
I lower myself to his lap,
slide the red rose
down one of his cheeks.

His hand
slips underneath my bottom
and squeezes.

I can feel his desire.

I rise
and hold the rose in front of him.
I begin to strip
each fragrant petal
from the flower
one by one.

They fall into his lap
in a pile.

You are the winner, Loredano.

But I'm sorry.

I cannot distribute the flowers,

*after I have already yielded
the fruit.*

A murmur arises in the audience.

My mother stands
and moves across the room.

What are you doing, Barbara?

I'm sorry, Mother.

I walk to Nicolò
and stand next to him.

*The bloom
has already been plucked.*

Atto lets out a joyful whoop.

Ferrante
reaches down
his leg
and draws a dagger
from his boot.

Holds it out
in a pathetic display.

You little whore!

I scan the audience.

The looks of shock and awe.
Disappointment.

I turn,
and run.

I run through the winding alleyways

I find a dark corner to hide in.
Sit on the ground.

Hug my knees to my chest.

I am alone on a boat
in the middle of the sea.

There is no one coming to save me.

What have I done?

The magnitude
hits me in waves of nausea.

The sun is setting.

Finally I stand.

I need Nicolò.
He'll help me.

We'll make a plan.

Together.

Ferrante steps out of the shadows

Ah . . . yes.

I thought I would find you here.

I can see
Nicolò's doorway
in the distance.

I feel my stomach turn.
The bottom drops out.

I always knew you were a slut.

The edges of my vision
go black and blurry
with fear.

*You just needed a little time
to step into your mother's
very worn shoes.*

He snickers at his own joke.

I can't think.
I can't run.

He's got me trapped
in the corner of the courtyard.

Hasn't it all been leading to this?

*Since that first moment
in the alleyway?*

> *You spilled your fruit,*
> *and I knew*
> *eventually the time would come*
> *to sample the sweetness.*

He edges closer.
I back up but hit the wall.

> *Isn't this*
> *what you've always wanted?*

He leans to kiss me,
and I shove him away.

He sneers.

> *I'm so turned on*
> *by the fight in you.*

Leave me alone, Ferrante!
I spit.

I have never wanted you.
I will never want you.

> *Ah, yes,*

he says, and steps closer.

> *But you do want*
> *our dear, poor, destitute Nicolò.*

> *Shame he doesn't have a penny to his name.*

He has more worth
than you ever will.

He shoves me to the wall.

Grabs me hard
in the center of my legs.

I gasp in pain.

Does he fill you up?

Does he make you gasp?

He traps me with his weight
and grinds his hips into me.

With pleasure?

He wraps one hand around my neck
and pushes so hard,
I can't breathe.

With pain?

He grabs my bodice and rips it.

My breast is exposed.
He grabs it hard.

Digs his fingernails
into my flesh.

I can feel him swell.
A jagged dagger.

*Loredano may let this pass,
but I always collect
what I am owed.*

It's long overdue.

He smashes his lips against mine
grabs my hips
and thrusts his tongue
into my mouth.

I shove him hard.
He does not falter.

He looks me in the eyes.

You still don't understand how this works, do you?

He punches me in the face.

The back of my head ricochets
off the brick.

My head buzzes I can't hear waves I can't feel

my body. I am dispersed into dust glimmer light. I try to focus my
eyes there is nothing. Only a bright star and the salt shining in
the moonlight on the bricks. The bells are ringing. The bells. The
lantern sputters like a blinking eye through the labyrinth. The canal
is green and turquoise and the light shines through. I want to swim
underneath the waters leave my human form join the brave and
dangerous women who breathe underwater I can hear the sirens
sing a song for all the souls lost at sea chaos of the waves chaos
of the black murky blood water I can hear the bells I fear I may
never return I am lost there is no home I do not have legs I am
made of waves spitting with foam I cannot stand please don't make
me please don't do this I am being split into two splintered wood
shattered glass she sings reach for my hand I can see her auburn
hair waving in the water there is a knife go further down into the
dark waters sister reach a star shines through the darkness you can
reach it if you try breathe underwater the weight will not crush you
breathe in and out be strong where are you god I want my body
back hear me singing for you I am singing myself *home home home*

(DUET)

Bells:

        a burst of dissonance
                      metallic shock
     resounding
              tintinnabulation
you ring us
     in union
                      you ring us
  in death
        in prayer
          in love
    we announce
              the morning
  the night
      two singing
    bodies
       in one tower
ringing
                    separate
   together
      separate
             together
      together
      together
  at the same time

(CHORUS)

Magic:

a dream

a spell

can you hear the bells?

a finger tip

the water dips

look deeply into mine

let me show you

a slip

through time

26
Lula

Venice, Italy
2025

Home

I whisper again,
my hand still resting on the doorknob.

Barbara's front door.

Bells and sirens ringing in my ears.
The water is rising.

The city is flooding.

My mind blurs.

The bells.

The wind pulls at my clothing.
I can barely keep my feet on the ground.

Water rushes onto the sidewalk,
seeps across the concrete,
fills the courtyard.

The ocean and the city
become one
glistening surface of light and water.

Water rises to my calves.

I can't tell where the canal begins,
where the concrete ends.

Buildings reflecting in the water.

I see starlight and moonlight.
Rain and tides.

The bells.

The bells.

Everything blends into a circle of black.

I'm so dizzy.
I'm spinning.
The reflection.
The water.

Which way is up?
Which was is down?

My ears are ringing

My eyes can't focus.
I can't clear my head.
Lula? Are you okay?
I can hear Cass, but I can't focus.
I keep walking. Yes . . . but I can't.

I feel so dizzy.
A ship that's turning in the ocean.
Vertigo waves cresting the sides.
I hear singing. It's so loud.
The bells, and the voices.
There's someone crying.
Home.

Lula. Do you need to sit down?
My eyes are blurring.
I keep walking. I stumble.
On all fours, staring into water.

I see a woman swimming.
Her dark hair floating around her face.
We are mirrored images.
Reaching for each other.
Bodies extended. Floating in the reflection.
She's singing to me.
Home.

There's something glinting in the water.
I see a knife. She needs me to hand her the knife.

Lula! The tide is rising.
This is getting dangerous.
We need to go.

I lean farther.
My arm submerged in the water.
She needs me, I whisper.

Who? Who are you talking about?
Lula! Are you hallucinating?
You're going to fall in!

He grabs my shoulder.
I push him away.
I can save her.

I dive in.
A siren. A song.

I plunge into the cold water

sink down into the dark.
The water holds me.
I am surrounded by singing.
Light swirling at the surface.
I swim toward her,
through a tunnel.
The knife in my hand.

26
Barbara

Venice, Italy
1635

I reach

while he's lost in me

I reach

down the side of his bare leg

I reach

for the hand
of my sister,

a glinting star

I reach
through the water

I reach

for something I know
is there

I reach

cold hard
shimmering
steel

I slide it
from its sheath

I reach

my hand high above
no longer human
a siren
I bare my sharp teeth
defending
and singing

I stab Ferrante
with the blade

as hard
as I can.

(CHORUS)

The Mother:

it is time

swim to the surface

the opening

to the one

who has always

been with you

sang to you

while you grew

your bones and sinew

muscles to move

a beating heart

breathe

breathe

breathe

27
Lula

Venice, Italy
2025

With bursting lungs

I pump my arms through water, muscles,
mouth open, screaming, I rise, bubbles forming,
bursting, pushing me to the surface, inhale,
my hands and mouth grasping for air, my lungs fill
with oxygen, every cell in my body rejoices.
I am alive.

I reach high above me

The edge of the canal.
I pull, but I can't lift my body to the rim.

Cass! I hear silence.
Then an echo.

I can't see him.

My body still submerged in the water.
The night sky is purple.
I can see lanterns, windows shining with light.

I'm shivering.
This water is so cold.

I wipe the canal from my eyes and try to focus.

What the hell.
Did I swim here?
Underwater?
Through a tunnel?

My heart is beating out of my chest.
I just kissed Cass.
Am I going to die here?
Before I get to kiss him again?

I need to get out of this water.
I'm freezing.

I use my whole body to shimmy along the side.
It's slippery and green with algae.

Where am I?
It looks like an alcove.
With four walls made of brick.

I look at my hands.
Am I still holding a knife?

Barbara?
I ask with a small, soft voice.

I must be in shock.
From the cold.
Did I die?

I let go of the side and swim farther out,
try to see where I am.

There's an outline of two poles.
I swim closer, and I can see an old staircase,
crumbling into the water.

I found an entryway.
I see lights from within the building.
Reach the stairs.

Climb up on my hands and knees.
Pull myself onto the landing.

Roll onto my back and breathe.

I stare at the black ink of night

I'm out of the water.
Sit up and look at my surroundings.
I'm in a little lagoon.

How could I have gotten here?
Did I swim under a wall?

There's a massive carved wooden door
in front of me with a large brass handle
with a hole in the middle.

I turn the handle to see if it opens,
but the door doesn't budge.

I feel the key hanging on the chain from my neck.
I chuckle.
Is it that easy?

I take it from my neck and try to shove it into the hole
and jiggle. It doesn't fit. Of course.
That would be too perfect.

I run my hands across the carvings on the door.
They feel ancient.
Spirals and swirls, letters within the curves.
I close my eyes.

Cass! I yell again, my voice ragged with fear.

I look around and squint

I can see lights in the building.
Someone must be home.

Is there a doorbell?
Should I just pound with my fists
until they let me inside?

I run my hands along the door.
The stone wall beside it.

It's smooth and cold.
And then, my heart skips a beat.

No. It can't be. I lean down.
Focus my eyes.

I trace the carved circle with my finger.
Three crescent moons.

A heart in the middle.

It's the symbol on my ring.

Heart on fire

The key slides through your fingers.

I slide the ring off my finger

Push it into the large brass handle.
I turn it to the left.
The door clicks open.

27
Barbara

Venice, Italy
1635

I wake

Pool of blood.

Ripped and torn.

Alone.

I hear someone moaning.

I hear myself weeping.

Push against the wall.

Get to my feet.

Vomit.

Feel the back of my head.

Crusted red.

Stains my fingers.

Slide my hand on the brick.

Walk.

Foot in front of the other.

Take a breath.

All pain.

Everywhere pain.

The alley.

The printer shop.

Climb steps.

Fall against door.

Door opens.

Nicolò

My beloved Nicolò.

I fall forward.
Reach for him.

> *Barbara!*
> *Oh my God!*
>
> *You're bleeding!*

He walks me to the bed.
Kneels beside me.

And that's when I see them.

Loredano and Ferrante
standing
in the corner.

Loredano
looking entertained
by the chaos.

The devil
staring into a flame.

Oh my, Barbara!

Loredano laughs.

He is amused.

> *I'm all for women's independence.*

> *But today!*

> *You really showed us
> what you're made of!*

> *You're a living opera!*

I'm trying to focus,
but there are two of him.

I'm afraid
I'm going to vomit again.

> *Look what you did to Ferrante.*

I look again,
and see a dirty sling
across Ferrante's shoulder.

Pale, sallow skin,
cheeks and hands
covered in my blood.

His hands fisted.
Silent.
Rage.

Loredano continues,

> *Who would have ever guessed!*

> *A kitchen maid with such pizazz!*

> *It's been a pleasure to watch you grow.*

I bob and sway.

Nicolò.

I'm going to black out.

Nicolò,
I need to go home.

Please take me home.

> *Nicolò will not be going anywhere.*

Nicolò.

I search for his green eyes.
Shining like the lagoon.

Swimming water.

Siren's home.

But his eyes are
dark, and I cannot find
the water's light
in them.

Nicolò.

Help me.

He rises to his feet.

Without a word,
he opens the front door,
gestures down
the long, steep stairway.

Head down.
Eyes on the floor.

28
Lula

Venice, Italy
2025

The hallway is dark

Objects like that, passed from one generation to another, hold a lot of power and history.

It smells like cold and stone.
I run my hand along the side of the wall,
walking toward a flickering light.

They are often keys to our past.

There's singing in the distance.
I walk farther down the corridor.

Two gigantic doors carved with shining stars
that look like the inside of shells.
Mother-of-pearl.
Hanging from the branches of a colossal tree.

You must pass through the willow tree.

I press hard on the doors.
They creak and resist, then begin to move.

My hungry eyes

focus on the immense room before me.

Candlelight flickers against walls
of books stacked on dark wooden shelves.

Floor-to-ceiling stained-glass windows
and spiraling staircases.

A library, I whisper.

An old woman approaches me

She's wearing a red veil, embroidered dress,
a diamond-shaped belt.
She takes both of my hands, and asks,
Why have you come?

I stumble over my words. *I don't know.*
I fell into the water.

She looks at my wet clothes and calls
to a younger woman in a language
I don't recognize.

The younger woman is wearing the same veil,
the same embroidered dress.
She has dreadlocks and a spiral necklace.

It's you, I sputter.
You're the woman from the museum.

She drapes a red blanket over my shoulders.

I wondered if you would find your way here.
She chuckles.
I see you learned how to use your key.

She hands me a mug full of warm liquid, sweet and spicy.
I take a sip and it coats my throat
with a numbing sensation.

The older woman takes my hand again,
runs her thumb over my ring.
The red stone and the gold band.

I haven't seen one of these in a very long time,
she says, in a soft voice.

Are you searching for something?

The older woman asks, and looks at me
with intention.
I shrug my shoulders.
I don't know.

She sits beside me.
Waiting.

I don't know why I'm here, I say again.

She closes her eyes in meditation,
lips moving in a chant I don't understand.

Something inside me shifts.

I look around and see pillars of a temple built long ago.

*She is the great decider of who will be allowed to cross
between earth and the afterlife, and who will walk between.*

The water, the singing, the searching.
The ring.

I look at the stacks of books, the stories,
the history, the women who have protected
this space, kept it safe and sacred.

*The sanctuaries built in her honor
invoked the protection of the goddess,
offered miracles and hope.*

Goddess of the earth and body. Goddess of writing.
Goddess of music. Goddess of healing.

I know where I am.

I know why I am here.

I'm broken

I say out loud.
Tears streaming down my cheeks.
I need help.

She wipes the tears from my eyes.
We are all broken in some way.

She stands up and helps me to my feet.
When something is broken, it does not make it less beautiful.

We walk together up the stairs to the second level.
She looks at the key hanging around my neck.
She touches it, smiles, and pulls a similar one
from under her tunic collar.

Sometimes the broken cracks let the light shine through.
She opens a small door in a bookcase,
and motions for me to step inside.

There's a staircase

I walk ahead of her and look back.
You're not coming with me?
She shakes her head.
Some things we must do alone.
Take all the time you need.

28
Barbara

Venice, Italy
1635

After hours of wandering

Walking.
Vomiting.
Falling.
Blackness.
Darkness.

I see a lantern lit
by the doorframe

I know so well.

My mind numb
with the horrible question.

Will they let me inside?

I collapse

with a thump
against the wood.

The door opens
and I fall inside.

Someone is screaming.

I'm lost in a swirl,
the tide.
An eddy pulls me under
and there is only
black.

I feel someone lifting me

I smell the tang of alcohol on my wounds
I taste warm tea on my tongue
I hear the bathwater being poured

I feel my dress being lifted from my body
I smell my mother's hair
I taste blood
I hear crying

I feel my skin being tugged by a needle
I smell lavender soap and water
I taste Rossini's warm soup
I hear my name called over and over

I feel my breath, in and out
I smell clean sheets
I taste olive oil smoothed on my lips
I hear the siren singing for me

I wake

My mother and signore
are by my bed.

Holding my hands.

I can't speak.

I'm filled with
relief
shame
anger
sadness
humiliation.

Rossini and Mancini
arrive.

They sit by the bed too.

They are all here.

I am home.

I'm so sorry

for what I have done.

I embarrassed you.

I brought shame to the household.

My voice cracks.
I can't look them in the eye.

My mother
squeezes my hand.

> *No, Barbara.*

> *I am sorry.*

> *I thought this was the best choice.*

> *I thought I was protecting you. . . .*
> *Now I see . . .*

Signor Strozzi
looks at my mother.

> *There is nothing more important to me*
> *than Isabella.*

Then looks at me.

> *And you.*

He places his hands
on his heart.

> *I am not your father,*
> *but I wish I could be.*

He closes his eyes for a moment,
as a tear slides down his cheek.

Takes a breath,
opens his eyes,
and says,

> *Sei la mia figliuola elettiva.*
> *You are my chosen daughter.*
>
> *I want you to know*
> *that I have changed my will.*
>
> *I want you both*
> *to have all that I have.*
>
> *I want us*
> *to be a family.*

My mother's mouth drops open.

> *Giulio,* she whispers.
> *I don't know what to say.*

Signore looks at me,
with eyes that are soft and hopeful.
Full of emotion.

I want to hate him.

I want to slap his face,
for what he has done to me,
but also, I know,
I've spent years admiring this man.

Loving this man.

Listening at the keyhole,
while he filled the house with music.

My only father figure.

Wishing he would see me.
Educate me.
Love me in return.

Now I know he does.

My heart fills

with forgiveness.

I reach for my mother's hand.

Her story.
Her scars.

She has made me strong.

I reach for Giulio's hand too.

Ti amo, I say,
as the tears fall.

29

Lula

Venice, Italy
2025

The spiral staircase is filled with shadows

My eyes adjust.
I arrive at the top and see a windowed turret,
with a view of the rooftops.
There are ancient paintings on the walls.
Spirals and keys, depictions of Reitia,
the mother goddess, surrounded by water and trees.
Shelves and glass cases hold drawings
and votives, offerings.
There is a shelf lined with many cups and vessels.
I drain my glass and add mine to the others.
A testament to those who have visited before me.
I run my fingers across the statues,
feel the carvings of the ancient ruins.
There are dishes of water, marking
north, south, east, west.
Lit candles and flowers floating in the pools.
I know I'm supposed to leave an offering.
I search my pockets.
I have nothing.
I sit in the center of the circle of candles.
Surrounded by the smell of wood and metal,
burning flames and flowers.
My eyes close.
I lie down on the floor and wait.

It begins with a sound

A low moan. A rattle. A shaking sigh.
The scream I left in the water.
Slick green sludge and shifting sand.
The years of grieving.
Dark and deep.
Impenetrable. I am there.
I am stuck in the mud.
Lying on the floor.
In this temple.
Fighting.
Lungs, diaphragm, abdomen bursting.
Full and tight.
Breathe in.
I can feel it.
I can push against the weight.
Breathe in.
I can release myself.
I can open my throat.
Air rushes through.
A bubble of pain rising
breaks through dark waters,
swimming to the surface.
My love, my strength,
my offering,
my voice.

I wake

my cheeks covered in tears.
I fell asleep in the library.
It's darker now.
The last of the candles flicker.
Cass.
He must be so worried.
How will I find my way back to him?
I stand and place my hand
on a carved bench to lift myself up.
My fingers drum against the wood.
I knock again. It's hollow.
I run my hands along the rim,
and lift.

There are many things inside

Fabric and furs. Jewelry and vases.
Pictures of children. Books.
Locks of hair. Coins.
Statues. Letters and cards.
One thing catches my eye.
A stack of paper wrapped in red ribbon.
Musical notes swimming
along the canal of a musical staff.
A letter attached.

My star,

I do not know if you were
a specter, or a vision,
but I know
you were there.

A light
surrounded by darkness,
you moved
through the water.

You heard me singing.

In my sorrow,
I reached for you.

You gave me the courage
to know
what must be done.

I leave you this gift
to find.

In your own time.

Bring me
wherever your journey
takes you.

No matter the cost,
the danger,
the fear.

It is time to be free.

Take my voice
and make it yours.

~Barbara Strozzi

(CHORUS)

Voice:

center yourself

fill your body

stretch the bones

of your spine

with life

break the bonds

that hold you here

breathe out

breathe in

open yourself

to the divine

this is how the music

begins

29
Barbara

Venice, Italy
1635

While my wounds heal

I write songs with my father.

It feels bizarre
to call him that,
but nice too.

We sit at the harpsichord for hours

He writes poetry,
song lyrics,
notes on scraps of paper.

Paces the room
in his dressing gown,
scratching his head,
gazing out the window.

Until he hops
on one foot
and writes another line.

I compose the music
on my lute.

I know at some point
I will have to see the men
of the academy.

Will they accept me
as my father's daughter?

I push the worries
into the notes
cascading
from my mouth
in song.

My father closes his eyes,
and bows his head.

The corners of his
lips lift.

I feel
gratitude and love
in his smile.

When I am alone

I speak to the siren

who lives within
my bones

she sings me down
a tunnel

beyond the deepest
ocean

into the earth

all the love
all the pain
all the anger
all the violence

prayers of hope
and joy

live in this music

these are the songs
that need
to live

in the world

but come
from the spirit.

30

Lula

Venice, Italy
2025

The woman in the red veil leads me

out of the library
into a courtyard, filled with lush ferns,
purple thistle, and blooming
bellflowers.

I close my eyes and breathe in the green.

The first light of morning is
scattering across the sky.

There are two ways into the library, she explains.
The canal is the hardest. But you managed that.
I twist my ring on my finger and smile.

The other is a secret passageway
through this wall. You just need to know where to push.
She curls her lips with pride,
moves aside a vine, and pushes a point on the wall,
and the door unlatches.

I look at the outside of the door.
It's covered in graffiti art.
A willow tree painted on the bricks.

Devi passare attraverso la porta di salice.

You must pass through the willow tree.

Of course, I laugh, *of course.*
I wipe tears from my eyes.

I would have found this place
one way or another.

Lula! Lula!

There are voices coming from the alleyway.

Looks like your friends are searching for you,
the woman says, and grins.

I don't know how to thank you, I whisper,
and hug her tightly.

I hold up the manuscript. *I can bring this back.*

It belongs to you.
She places her palms together, presses them
to her forehead and then her heart.

I follow the voices

take two turns, wading through the canal water
still pooled on the concrete.

Cass sees me, and runs,
splashing water with each step.
Grabs me and pulls me into his chest.

Jesucristo, he whispers. *Gracias, Maria, madre de Dios.*

I place one hand on his cheek.
Cass, are you praying? He's crying.

Don't ever disappear again, he says,
and kisses me hard on the lips.

Whoa, Nellie. Agatha chuckles and hugs us both.
I laugh and say, *This is a new thing we do.*

Cass responds, *We're going to be doing this A LOT.*
He kisses me again.

I see Cynthe, Madison, and Jenkins.
Brick peeks out from a corner
and waves.

Jenkins works her way through the group.
She's weeping.
My turn, she yelps.
We were so worried. I'm so glad you're okay.

She wipes her tears and adds,
AND thank GOD
I don't have to call your mother.

I have something to show you

I walk under the portico and pull out the manuscript.
Jenkins looks at the package. The ribbon. The note.

Lula. Is this what I think it is? I nod.

She doesn't say anything,
just flips through the pages.
It can't be.

I look at her and smile.
I think I found our last song.

Jenkins shakes her head.
*I told you Barbara has a way of choosing the people
who need her the most.*

She hugs me tight.

Then she straightens her spine,
looks at the group, lifts the manuscript.

We have work to do!

The phone rings twice

Lula?
I can hear her breathing.
Worried something is wrong.
Shocked it's me.

Hi, Mom.
There's silence.

Do you need to come home?
Are you hurt?

I'm okay.
I look down at my feet.

How can I tell her about the fall?
The library.
The sound that escaped from me.
The lost manuscript.

There's music in the background.

Cass is smiling at me, leaning
against a large marble arch.

Agatha is dancing around Cynthe,
her scarves floating in the air
like butterfly wings.

Jenkins is sitting, eyes closed,
listening to the music.

Mom . . .
I just wanted to tell you . . .
I love you.

Silence.
Mom? Can you hear me?

Her voice soft and tender.
I love you too, Lula.

I can hear her breathe in.
She's waiting for me to speak.

I think about the expectations.
The emotions.
The anger. The fear.
Afraid I would never be good enough.

The pressure she put on me.
The pressure I put on myself.

I think about all the time she gave me.
All the sacrifices.

I've tried so hard to be perfect, Mom.

The emotion catches in my throat.

I'm exhausted.

Lula, are you okay?
My mom's voice wavers.

She takes a deep breath.
You don't have to be perfect.
I just want you to be happy.
And . . . healthy.

I close my eyes, and let her words sink in.

I'm going to try. . . .

I have to go now.
We're rehearsing.

Tears fall down my cheeks,
and I wipe them away with my sleeve.

I just needed to hear your voice.

The line goes silent.

Then for the first time
in a very long time

I hear her laugh.

Bring the house down, Lula-belle.

30
Barbara

Venice, Italy
1635

The autumn has passed

The first dusting of snow
is on the ground.

I can hear the tingling of bells
ringing on the carts
clattering over the cobblestone.

I reach for a blanket
to wrap around my shoulders,
when there's a knock
at the door.

Rossini rushes to get it,
but I hold my hand up.
Allow me.

She smiles and bows.

When I open the door,
I gasp.

Bright blue eyes
smoldering
amid dark features.

A mop of curly
black hair.

A man,
holding a bouquet
of dried lavender.

Are those for Signor Strozzi?

I smile politely.

He blushes,
and says,

> *These are for you.*
>
> *Someone once told me,*
> *lavender flowers represent*
> *desire.*

His voice has an accent.

Different from any
I have ever heard.

Ah!
She must have been
the goddess Flora!
I say.

She left a while ago,
and hasn't returned.

I shiver
in the cold air.

> *No.*
> *Not Flora.*
> *But a goddess nonetheless.*

He blushes again.

> *My name is*
> *Giovanni Paolo Widmann.*

He clears his throat.

> *Count Widmann.*

I stop smiling.

My heart is beating
in my throat.

> *I wish to tell you*
> *that I wanted the rose,*
> *but I did not pay for it.*
>
> *For I believe a woman*
> *must give herself freely.*

My chest tightens.
I feel faint.

I reach
for the doorframe
to steady myself.

> *I am here,*
> *and I would like to offer you*
> *anything you need.*

He hands me the bouquet.

 Or desire.

When our hands meet,
I feel a shock
run from my neck
all the way down
my spine.

I raise my eyebrows,
lower my chin,
and look up at him.

*I'll let you know
if I can think of something.*

My cheeks
and breasts flush
with heat.

His sky-blue eyes
rise to the heavens,
as if praying,
then return to me.
He bows.

 I'm at your disposal.

Then he smiles a shy grin.

 Day or night.

(CHORUS)

Music:

rough paper

deep black ink

soaked into the fiber

lines and circles

rhythm and notes

punctuated by legato

and staccato

points

this silent object

a map

of sound and power

contained

waiting

for the moment

the right voice

to set it

free

31
Lula

Venice, Italy
2025

The Greenroom

Every performance begins with a moment of reflection.
Staring into the mirror, just me and the lights.
Here in this cathedral, I realize,
there has been an ache living in my heart,
and now it's gone.
Agatha and Cass and Cynthe wave at me.
They tune their instruments, listening to each other.
We've been up all night rehearsing.
We're exhausted and excited.
Professor Jenkins places her hand on my shoulder.
She gives me a smile that shatters my fear.
The audience has gathered.
I can hear the footsteps.
Everything feels as if it has fallen into the exact right place.
The light beam angling from the stained-glass window.
The chalky dust swirling in the light.
The only place that matters is here.
Right now. This cathedral. This moment.
With my beloved friends and teacher.

The group takes the stage

They perform the pieces
they have been working on for weeks.

My eyes fill with tears
when Madison and Brick sing
"Bist du bei mir," so soft, so sweet.

The sound lifts and joins the color
streaming down from
the stained-glass windows.

Jenkins directs the ensemble,
smiling at each triumph.

Finally it's my turn to join them.
I step onto the stage,
and fight to find the courage to speak.

Our last piece
is an unknown song by Barbara Strozzi,
recently discovered in an archive in Venice.

The crowd gasps.

The space fills with whispers.
Questions floating in the air.

It's a new arrangement.

I had to imagine, in a very short time,
what she would have wanted us to play.
I had to imagine what she would have wanted
you to hear.

I pause, fear filling my heart.
I can't find my breath.

My throat is tightening.

Jenkins searches for my eyes.
She drops her chin, raises her eyebrows,
looks at me. Hard.

Full of support and love. Courage.

I speak again.

When I sing this song,

I am not singing with my voice alone.

I carry all the women
who have come before me.

Who have risen from their knees.

Healed their wounds and carried on.

Women who have felt a spirit
so strong, so deep, they need to create
a song for the world.

When I stand here,
I am not just me.

I am filled with their love.

A hush

fills the cathedral.

A shiver runs up my spine.

My ears fill with the sound of water.

I dive down deep, into the darkness.

Floating. Waiting. Held.

Light swirling at the surface.

I ground my feet, center my spine.

Fill my lungs with air.

My body fills with breath, sound.

I am not alone.

I have never been alone.

Thanks to you, my star

My voice rings out.

Clear, strong.

I fill the space
with warmth and light.

Siamo stati incoronati dall'immortalità.

We have been crowned with immortality.

A single flame
glowing
through the shadow.

Che il difficile e il bello abbiano inizio.

Let the difficult and beautiful commence.

Madison steps forward and grabs my hand.
Our voices join,
weaving in and out.

*Un canto gioioso, ha intrecciato i nostri cuori
uniti dalle nostre voci.*

*A joyful song, intertwined our hearts,
united by our voices.*

Our flame grows brighter,
fills the darkness.

The audience leans forward.

Jenkins nods to the group
and Cass, Agatha, and Cynthe
join us.

With closed eyes, power, and precision,
they strike the notes, filled with emotion.

Madison and I
sing in full voice, together.

Two bells ringing side by side.

Filling the cathedral with resonance.

>   *Che dolce armonia creano due anime fedeli.*

What sweet harmony two faithful souls make.

I sing without pain.

Without fear.

My light shines from within.

>   *Guarigione gioia e risate.*

>   *Una canzone.*

Healing joy and laughter.

A song.

I reach my hand out
into the darkness.

Into the depth.

I know she can hear me.
I know she is with me.

Finally singing
the words she wrote.

I cuori uniti dalla musica non moriranno mai.

Hearts brought together by music
will never die.

31
Barbara

Venice, Italy
1635

I run the tips of my fingers

across paper.

Follow the lines.
The formed notes.

Scattered stars,
across the open page.

I tap two different manuscripts
on the table.

The edges are even and neat.

Wrap
the separate piles
each with its own ribbon,
so they won't be
swept away
by the wind.

Tie my hair
with a piece of the same ribbon.

Place both parcels
under my arm,
and walk
to Nicolò's apartment.

I gaze at the stairway

where he once kissed my lips
as if they were
cherished.

The stairway

I walked alone,
yearning, strong,
and hungry.

My body.
My heart.

The stairway

where he left me.

Bleeding,
blind.

Punished.

For giving him
everything.

Alone.

Trying to find home.

I gaze at the stairway.

And I know
one thing
has not changed.

I am still betting
on myself.

I turn

and open the door
to the left.

It smells like
metal and grease,
motion
and collision,
body
and blood.

Moveable type
pressed
into soft,
impressionable
paper.

A man wearing an apron
looks up
from his work.

His wire-rim glasses
slide to the end
of his nose.

 Can I help you, signorina?

 Ah!

 *Aren't you a friend
 of Nicolò's?*

I nod,
and clear my throat.

My father,
Giulio Strozzi,

*hopes that you would be willing
to publish
this manuscript.*

 Signor Strozzi?

I hand him
one of the two
stacks of paper
that I am holding.

 Signorina.

 *I'm sorry, we cannot
 accept everything. . . .
 We can only accept the finest—*

Please, can you look at it?

I promise, I will leave
if you do not see any merit
in the work.

He pushes
his glasses up his nose
with his forefinger.

Takes the manuscript
to a harpsichord.

Sits down to read.

Fingers tap
across the keyboard.

He looks up and asks,

 Did your father compose these?

He wrote the lyrics.

I straighten my spine.

I am the composer.

    A woman composer?

I am a composer.

And I am a woman.

I raise my chin.

I studied with Cavalli.

    Cavalli?
Yes.

    Maestro Cavalli?

I nod.

I want to publish my work.

    Why?

I ball my fingers
into fists,
and breathe.

Close my eyes for a moment.

Calm.

So I can be independent.
So I can earn a living.
So I can be heard.
So people will know my name.
So I can be remembered.

    And your father agrees?

He will agree.

There is a long pause.

The printer's
eyeglasses
slowly
slide down
his nose again.

    I will print this.

My heart
pounds
out of my chest.

    With conditions.

My stomach
drops.

What will he ask of me?

My body?
My freedom?
Credit for my work?

I cannot . . .
I will not . . .

> *Payment will be received
> after I sell fifty copies.*

You're going to publish my work?

> *Yes.*

You're going to sell my work?

> *Yes.*

> *I will TRY
> to sell your work—
> to my regular customers.*

> *We will see if they like it.*

> *If they do,
> I will pay you for the copies sold,
> and we can talk
> about publishing more.*

You want to publish more?

> *Don't get ahead of yourself.*

He chuckles
and walks me to the door.

> *Let's take this
> one manuscript at a time,
> signorina.*

My next stop is the library

I walk there
holding the second manuscript
close to my chest.

Place my mother's ring
on my finger.

Insert it into the keyhole,
twist, and hear it
click.

I walk toward the door.

Push hard
on the shining
willow tree.

I stand in the middle
of the cavernous room.

Filled with the words,
thoughts, and history
in each of these books.

I can hear the voices singing
through the pages.

I drop to my knees,
dip my forehead
to the cold, mosaic,
marble floor.

My chest swells with emotion.

I am safe here.

A woman

kneels beside me.

Her hair is covered
in a red veil.

She places her hand
on my back.

> *Are you well,*
> *my child?*

Tears stream down my cheeks.

No.
But I am trying to be.

She nods
with understanding.

I take the manuscript
from under my arm.

I have an offering.

(CHORUS)

Time:

light fades
tide recedes
wind pounds against the windows
whistles through the hallways
the pages
flutter
rain batters
granite walls
a library
the moon glows
pulls
tide rises
lifts boats
fills estuaries
the streets with high water
a tree glows
the pearl of night
a star
shadows shift
sand
softens stone
edges
shapes coastlines
the canal
blends into the water
a cove
a lagoon forms
the entrance
disappears

(FINALE)

We remember

the stories
calling
through years

We remember

the untold

We remember

the wounds
the buried bones
the unmarked graves

We remember

those who lived
those who fought
those who thrived

We remember

the damaged
the helpless
the searching

We remember

the love
the longing
the lasting

We remember you.

ACKNOWLEDGMENTS

This book would not have been published without a mountain of support from my village of colleagues, friends, and family.

First and foremost, thank you, Jen Henderson. You read every version of this book, and let me obsess about every detail, helped me work through all the gnarly and tangled bits through our weekly (sometimes daily) calls, and you edited all the descriptions and pitches with aplomb. Thank you for being an amazing writing partner.

Thank you to all my evergreen students and besties—Annie Battle, Martha Blandford, Stéphanie Larotte-Namouni, Barbara Tennis, Barbara Cole-Kiernan, Fran Swart, Hope Cotter, Sondra Scott, (and Jen Henderson again). I thank the goddess for you.

Thank you to the Creative Coven (Jessica Pearce Rotondi, Amy Jo Burns, Yoojin Grace Wuertz, Caitlin Mullen, Lauren Keating, Laura Spence-Ash, and Millie Chandler), a badass group of authors who help me to create books, process life, be a mom, cry, and then create again.

Thank you, Anica Mrose Rissi, for the meadow tromps, porch hangs, and deep, heartfelt talks about life and craft. I'm so happy to be walking down this writerly path with you.

Thank you to the Princeton Poets (Megan Cho, Chris Munford, Michael Dickman, and Patrice Alan Nganang) for keeping me on my toes, and delving into the often dizzying world of poetry, and reminding me of the power of language.

Thank you to all the folks who read early drafts of this book. Rebecca Caprara and Kip Wilson, I could not have made it here without your first reads. You are both incredible writers and critique partners. I am continuously inspired by your talent.

Thank you to Kate Elliot, Helen Corveleyn, Clara Morgan, Charlotte Rowe, Hope Cotter, Mama Schoene-Langohr for all your loving insights and early reads.

Thank you to Dr. Robert B. Schoene and Dr. Stéphanie Larotte-Namouni for being my medical readers; Carolann Buff, Jessica Flint Weiss, Leonard Kim, and Mimi Morris-Kim for being my music readers; and Matteo Detto for helping with the Italian phrasing.

Thank you to Ms. Rochon, Ms. Schubin, Mr. Schubin, Mr. White, Mr. Kelly, and Ms. Cook for all the inspiring work that you do with the kids in the Hopewell Valley School District music and theater program. Watching you all rock as mentors, artists, and coaches inspires me every day, and has changed our life as a family.

Thank you, Dr. Lynell Jenkins. My kids have loved being your choir students. Naming a musicologist "Professor Jenkins" just sounded right! And thank you to my loving sister-in-law, Patience Schoene, for inspiring the name for Lula's ever-patient therapist.

Thank you, Hildegard von Blingin, for inspiring the Zuzu Restaurant scene, and for medieval-izing the lyrics to these beloved songs. Your music helped me bring these nerdy baroque kids to life.

Erin Cohn. Thank you for being my life partner in a best-friend package. You are the wisest, smartest, most kick-ass person I know. You can reframe the hell out of any problem, and you make me pee my pants laughing. And thanks for introducing me to the Kumquats, who are some of the smartest, deepest women I know.

Abigail Washburn and Kate Noson for your unending love, and for bringing me back into my body with your voices and music.

Paula Lampton and Wandee Pryor for reminding me who I am, and who I will be, and for being my favorite travel buddies.

Thank you, Barfinnschoenders, for being my backbone. Thank you for helping me laugh, cry, dance, and swim. Thank you, Ali Morgan, Debbie Reichard, Ellie Rock, Nicole Horlacher Robinson, Andrea Loftin, Emily Suzuki, Alanna Bocklage, and the Fanny Pack for being my most beloved village and keeping me grounded.

Thank you to my magnificent agent, Allison Hellegers, and Stimola Literary Studio. Alli—you and I know this book is going to live on the shelves of bookstores, libraries, and homes because you busted your butt to get it there. You are a brave, persistent, powerful woman, and I love you. Thanks for being my agent and my friend.

Thank you to my talented editor, Krista Vitola. When you first read this book, you said it was "kismet" that it found its way to you. I couldn't agree more. Thank you for all your insightful edits and camaraderie. This book truly wouldn't exist without your belief in the project. I will be forever grateful for you.

Thank you, Simon & Schuster Books for Young Readers, for producing such a gorgeous book. Thank you, Emma Leonard, for creating stunning artwork, and Krista Vossen for this glorious cover design. Thank you, Kimberly Capriola (managing editor),

Sara Berko (production manager), Bara MacNeill (copyeditor), and Kaitlyn San Miguel (proofreader). What a dream team! I couldn't imagine a better house for this book.

Okay, this is when I start to cry. Guys. I have the best kids. They were the first two people to read the manuscript. They read it all in one day, passing the pages between them. They barely ate. I loved listening to them giggle at the funny parts and get emotional and frustrated at the tough sections. Thank you, Bluebird and Sailboat, for the long walks and conversations about characters and plotting. It's not easy to have a mom who obsesses about the past, and lives in her imagination all the time. You are unendingly patient, supportive, creative, smart, loving, and fierce. I could not do this job if you weren't cheering me on.

Thank you to my mom, Jan, who loves to dance and sing, and took me to the opera and the theater at an early age. Our house was filled with art from around the world because of you.

And my dad, Jim, who from the earliest years would sit me on his lap, and hold a guitar against my belly, and sing me the saddest, sweetest songs. Long live Coco and the Pops.

Thank you to my sister, Darcy—the alto to my soprano—my best friend and lifelong duet.

Thank you to my forever love, Blair Schoene. You are *my noon, my midnight, my talk, my song*. Thank you for continuing to love me, after all these many years. You (and our beautiful children) are the reason I get up in the morning and keep writing.

And finally, thank you to every kid who wants to change the world with their art and music—it's possible, and your voice is needed now more than ever.

AUTHOR'S NOTE

When I started writing *The Siren and the Star*, I thought it was going to be a novel about Vivaldi. However, I soon realized I wanted to tell a story of a lesser-known voice and delve into a relatively unknown history. I wanted my book to be about a female composer.

I found Barbara Strozzi in a very similar way to how Lula found Barbara in the library at the New England Conservatory of Music. I asked for a sign. As I pursued my research, Barbara floated out of the ether and arrived in my life. I like to think she chose me, and I, in turn, chose her.

As a result, this book is filled with magic and connection and mystical thinking, and while I did use many real details about Barbara's life while weaving the story, I cannot stress enough that this novel is a work of fiction. To take you further into the story and my process, I would love to tell you more about my research, the characters, the historical events, my trip to Venice, and my inspiration.

My Research

I spent two years—even *before* I started writing—researching Strozzi, Venice, and baroque music.

I read many articles by scholars who have spent their lives studying Barbara and her music, including **Candace Magner, Ellen Rosand, Beth L. Glixon, Wendy Heller, Susan Mardinly, Sylvia Glickman, M. Schleifer,** and **Kathleen Ann Gonzalez.**

Most of the characters in Barbara's section of the story are inspired by historical figures. She and her mother, **Isabella Garzoni,** often referred to as **"La Greghetta,"** were servants in the Strozzi household, and she was later adopted by **Giulio Strozzi,** a famous librettist and a member of the **Accademia degli Incogniti (Academy of the Unknowns).** One thing that most scholars agree on is that Strozzi cared deeply for his adopted "chosen daughter," and in the words of scholar Ellen Rosand, in her groundbreaking work "Barbara Strozzi, *virtuosissima cantatrice*," Guilio Strozzi "intended to educate her and place her on the path of freedom" (Rosand 1981).

Strozzi encouraged Barbara as a musician. He sent her to study with the legendary Italian composer **Francesco Cavalli,** and created an organization—**Accademia degli Unison (Academy of the Like-Minded)**—to help her step out as a musician in society. Although many of the members were the same, the Unisoni were an offshoot of the Academy of the Unknowns. Please note that for the purpose of my book, I have combined the Incogniti and the Unisoni academies to keep the narrative flowing smoothly.

Giovanni Francesco Loredan (sometimes referred to as Loredano) was the head of the Academy of the Unknowns. He was a fascinating character that I could not quite fully understand—sometimes arguing for the rights of women and then simultaneously saying they were not equals. He wanted the academy to explore issues of war and love, the sacred and the sensual, gender and society. From what I could gather, Giovanni Francesco Loredan was complicated, calculating, layered, and mysterious.

Nicolò Fontei belonged to both academies and was one of Loredan's beneficiaries. He wrote a beautiful collection of music, *Bizzarrie Poetiche* (1635), found on BarbaraStrozzi.com, and in the dedication he states that his songs were inspired by "the most kind and virtuosic damsel, Signora Barbara." This collection of music inspired the relationship between Barbara and Nicolò in the book.

Ferrante is based on **Ferrante Pallavicino**, who, in my opinion, history shows to be an unsavory character. From what I could piece together, he was Giovanni Francesco Loredan's secretary, bookkeeper, and best friend. You can do your own research on him and his published works, but if you are still feeling angry about how Ferrante treated Barbara in this story, you will be interested to know that he was beheaded by the Papacy in Avignon, in 1644, at the age of twenty-eight.

Barbara did spend most of her adult life in a relationship with **Count Giovanni Paolo Widmann** (also spelled "Vidman" per BarbaraStrozzi.com), the handsome man who shows up at the end of the book. Although she never married him, or any other man, Barbara had four children. Widmann never gave his surname to any of her offspring, but his family acknowledged them *and* paid for their educations when they were grown. Her two daughters joined a convent, and one of her sons became a monk.

According to Beth Glixon in her paper "More on the Life and Death of Barbara Strozzi," a letter was written after Giulio Strozzi's death. The letter was penned by a mysterious "X" to "a man of the cloth" and reports that Barbara "was raped by Count Vidman, a Venetian nobleman, and had a son...." (Glixon 1999). This befuddles most who have studied Barbara. Many historians wonder why Widmann's name was put on the record, since by most accounts they seemed to have a consensual union for many years. Was it to justify an out-of-wedlock pregnancy, or to cover up their romantic affair, or to hide an attack by another man? We can't say for sure, but this was one of the unanswerable questions that inspired me to write this story.

Several of the scenes in the book were inspired by *Vegli de'Signori Unisoni* (1638) and *Satire, e altre raccolte per l'Accademia de gli Unisoni in casa di Giulio Strozzi* (1637), both of which detail many of the debates and meetings of the academy. Please see BarbaraStrozzi.com.

The **flower ceremony** is a fictional interpretation of an actual recorded event, where Barbara handed out flowers to the academy members. There are many different interpretations of this flower event, but I was inspired by Susan Mardinly and her PhD dissertation from the New England Conservatory of Music, "Barbara Strozzi and 'The Pleasures of Euterpe.'" Mardinly states that "Barbara honored Venus by portraying herself as Flora, patron of courtesans. Barbara distributed her flowers to her audience, thus lending substance to the view that the debates and musical sessions of the Unisoni were preludes to lovemaking. Consider what Sappho also writes: 'The plucking of blossoms . . . describe girls about to lose their virginity'" (Mardinly 2004).

This led me to wonder about Barbara's agency and free will during many of these academy gatherings. Was she the academy's pet? Was she a courtesan? Was she a well-respected woman equal to her male counterparts? How did the men of the academy view her, other than as a sensual siren who entertained them with her virtuosity? These are the questions that historical documents cannot fully answer.

The book *Satire, e altre raccolte per l'Academia de gl'Unisoni in casa di Giulio Strozzi* (1637) includes the slur, "It is a fine thing to distribute the flowers after having already surrendered the fruit," and I used this quote (found on BarbaraStrozzi.com) to inform the scene where Barbara is distributing flowers. I wondered, *How would Barbara have lost her virginity? Was it by choice? Was it forced? Was it transactional?*

This same satiric book includes another quote about Barbara's virtue: "To claim and to be chaste are very different; all the same, I too consider [Barbara] extremely chaste since as a woman with a liberal upbringing she could pass the time with some lover, yet she nevertheless concentrates all her affection on a castrato." This quote inspired the inclusion of Atto. I tried to find records with a castrato in this circle at this time and found the name **Adamo Franchi**, but I couldn't find a lot of material. So I modeled Barbara's best friend around the historical character **Atto Melani**, a castrato who at a young age sang at the Teatro Novissimo in Venice. Melani would have known the Strozzi family and worked closely with them.

When I decided to include Atto, I wanted to also reference the historical gender bending in seventeenth-century Venice that often happened—on and off the stage. Atto ended up being one of my favorite characters in the book, and I tried my hardest to relay the journey of a castrato during this period, with relevant historical details, respect, and sensitivity. I love the idea of Barbara and Atto relying on each other as they negotiated the libertine world filled with sexuality, art, power, and politics.

In the end Barbara really did get what I think she most desired—a house of her own, where she lived with her parents until Giulio passed, and then with her mother and Barbara's children. She wrote music and supported them with her publishing projects.

She published more music than any other woman—or any man!—in seventeenth-century Venice. She made so much money, in fact, that she even gave her father, and several other noblemen (including Widmann) loans with 10 percent interest! She was a powerhouse singer-songwriter and businesswoman who was way ahead of her time.

My Other Resources

If you want to delve into all the factual information about Barbara's life on record, here are a few more resources I found incredibly helpful.

Dr. Candace Magner has spent her life studying Barbara and cataloging her music, and she was extremely generous with her time while I was researching this book. Most of the lyrics in the book are adaptations and modernized lyrics from Candace's comprehensive archive at BarbaraStrozzi.com. Many of the songs that I included were from opuses that were written later in Barbara Strozzi's life (opus 7 and 8). I chose these songs because they fit with Barbara's and Lula's braided narrative, and I wanted to highlight a few of my favorites, even though they came after the book's timeline.

Also, the symbol on Barbara and Lula's ring came from a photo Dr. Magner took at the **Palazzo Strozzi in Florence** during one of her many research trips to Italy (see PalazzoStrozzi.org/en). It is a version of the Strozzi family crest, and the symbol for Dr. Magner's music-publishing business, **Cor Donato Editions** (CorDonatoEditions.com).

While I was researching and talking to historians, I discovered that there was a revival of ancient god/goddess worshipping during this era in Europe, and we see this in the prolific Greek god/goddess images that appear in much of the art during this time. In fact, the Academy of the Unknowns began each of their meetings with a dedication to *Ignotus Deus*, "the Unknown God." And in a bold feminist gesture, Barbara Strozzi dedicated opus 3 to *Ignotae Deae*, "the Unknown Goddess." I was intrigued by this idea, given the backdrop of the power of the papacy, the Counter-Reformation, and the libertine movement.

Because of this, I had planned to include **Reitia, a Veneto triple goddess**, worshipped during the Iron Age. I mean, she's the Venetian goddess of music, writing, and healing, so how could I *not* include her? And then I found out that the Strozzi crest had three crescent moons—the international symbol of the, you guessed it, *triple goddess*—and the connection seemed too perfect to be true. Talk about shivers up the spine.

If you want to learn more about Reitia, there's a museum near Venice, in Este, Italy, called the **Museo Nazionale Atestino** that has one of the largest holdings of Reitia artifacts (including the ones that I described in the story, in the museum in Venice).

Many of the details of Lula's trip came from my own research trip to Venice. Lula's outing in Venice was based on a day I spent with the lovely and talented musicologist **Mauro Masiero**. It was illuminating and inspiring to see Ca' Sagredo, the *scafetta* at the Ospedale della Pietà, and Chiesa di Santa Maria dei Derelitti through his eyes. I am grateful for his time. And thank you, **Diane Figarella**, who spent an afternoon with me talking about frescoes, palazzi, and baroque music halls.

I also learned about the natural phenomenon *acqua alta*, which describes the coalescence of the astronomical tide, a strong southern wind called sirocco, and Adriatic seiches. This flooding has been happening in Venice since the 700s, but it's getting worse due to climate change. Parts of the city flood over a period of several hours, and the population of Venice must wade through a pool of water that reflects the sky and the buildings and the lights. It's a magical, slightly dizzying, sometimes dangerous experience, and I thought the inclusion of this natural occurrence would be the perfect moment for Lula's and Barbara's physical worlds to collide. It also explains how the courtyard, and the entrances to the courtyard, could shift during this rising and falling of the tide.

My Real-Life Inspiration

When I was in Venice, I was given a **skeleton key** in the marketplace by a vendor! I'm still waiting to figure out what the key opens, so this mysterious talisman had to make an appearance in the book.

And yes, there really is a **lost manuscript** of Barbara's, and most historians believe it's waiting to be found—most likely in a library somewhere in Venice. When I first heard that, it made my entire body tingle. There's nothing like a lost manuscript to inspire years of research and international travel.

Mostly I want to tell you how inspired I was when writing this book. I fell in love with Barbara and wanted to learn everything that I could about her life. I loved thinking about her writing and composing, with her heart on fire, putting that passion onto the page. At a time when women had very few options, she created a life of her own. Maybe this book will encourage you to learn a little more about this incredible figure in music history. I truly hope it does.

Like Lula, I studied music for a lot of my life, singing in private girls' choirs, performing with the Minnesota Opera as a child at the Ordway Center for the Performing Arts (I was a child soldier in *Carmen*!), competing in vocal competitions, singing in bands with my best friends, and performing with an all-female a cappella group (shout-out to you, One Juicy Wedding Band and Ellement).

Music provided some of the most rewarding and challenging moments of my youth, and these experiences inspired me to write a character like Lula, who is searching for how to develop her talent, and wondering how to create art that lasts.

Just like Lula, when I got to Venice and walked through the labyrinth of alleyways and bridges, I didn't feel lost. And when I finally made my way to Barbara's house, and placed my hands on the stone, I felt like I was home.

I thank you, with all my heart, for reading this book. I hope you love Barbara and Lula's story as much as I do.

—Colby

WORKS CITED

Accademia degli Unisoni. Satire, e altre raccolte per l'Accademia de gli Unisoni in casa di Giulio Strozzi. Manuscript, Venice: Biblioteca Nazionale Marciana. I: Vnm Cl.X, Cod. CXV = 7193.

Accademia degli Unisoni. Veglie de' Signori Unisoni. (Veglia Prima; Veglia Seconda; Veglia Terza di Signori Accademici Unisoni) Venice: Sarzina, 1638. Located at Venice: Biblioteca Nazionale Marciana. I: Vnm 119 C 240.

"Bizzarrie Poetiche poste in musica." A 1.2.3 voci. Venice: Bartholomeo Magni, 1635. Notes: Dedicated to Giovanni Paolo Vidman. RISM F1485. GB: Och. I: microfilm

Glixon, Beth L. "More on the Life and Death of Barbara Strozzi." The Musical Quarterly, 83, no 1, Spring 1999, 134–141, https://doi.org/10.1093/mq/83.1.134.

Glixon, Beth L. "New Light on the Life and Career of Barbara Strozzi." The Musical Quarterly, 81, no 2, Summer 1997, pp.311–335

Magner, Candace, "A Brief History." 2020–2025, https://barbara.strozzi.com/a-brief-history/

Mardinly, Susan, "Barbara Strozzi and The Pleasures of Euterpe" (PhD diss., University of Connecticut, 2004), AAI3166003. https://digitalcommons.lib.uconn.edu/dissertations/AAI3166003.

Mardinly, Susan, "A "View" of Barbara Strozzi" IAWM, 15, no 2, 2009, pp.4–11

Rosand, David and Ellen, " "Barbara di Santa Sofia" and "Il Prete Genovese": On the Identity of a Portrait by Bernardo Strozzi." The Art Bulletin, 63, no 2, Jun 1981, pp.249–258

Rosand, Ellen, "Barbara Strozzi, "virtuosissima cantatrice," Journal of the American Musicological Society (1978) 31 (2): 241–281. https://doi.org/10.2307/830997.

ABOUT THE AUTHOR

Colby Cedar Smith is an award-winning poet, novelist, and educator. Her debut verse novel, *Call Me Athena: Girl from Detroit*, has been chosen as a Junior Library Guild Gold Standard Selection, an American Booksellers Association Indie Next List Pick, a Cybils Award Poetry Finalist, a Goodreads Choice Best Poetry Nominee, A Kids' Book Choice Nominee, an Independent Publisher Book Award, a Nautilus Book Award, a Michigan Notable Book, and the Midwest Book Award for YA Fiction. To learn more, visit ColbyCedarSmith.com or find her on Instagram @colby_cedar_smith.